spookily yours

jennifer chipman

To my spoopy, Halloween loving girlies.
This one's for you.

playlist

- willow - Taylor Swift
- Season Of The Witch - Lana Del Rey
- Lost - Michael Bublé
- I Put A Spell On You - Annie Lennox
- Make It To Me - Sam Smith
- A Safe Place to Land - Sara Bareilles, John Legend
- Wildest Dreams (Taylor's Version) - Taylor Swift
- Dancing With The Devil - Demi Lovato
- Through the Dark - One Direction
- Demons - Imagine Dragons
- Mercy - Lewis Capaldi
- ivy - Taylor Swift
- I Found - Amber Run
- Falling - Harry Styles
- If Only - Dove Cameron
- I Can See You - Taylor Swift
- MIDDLE OF THE NIGHT - Elley Duhé
- As Long As You're Mine - Stephen Schwartz, Idina Menzel
- Take Me To Church - Hozier

- I Don't Wanna Live Forever - ZAYN, Taylor Swift
- Love In The Dark - Adele
- Monster In Me - Little Mix
- exile - Taylor Swift, Bon Iver
- Graveyard - Halsey
- Die For You - The Weeknd
- Afterlife - Hailee Steinfeld
- Queen Of The Night - Hey Violet
- Sweater Weather - The Neighbourhood
- Hold Me While You Wait - Lewis Capaldi
- peace - Taylor Swift
- My Girlfriend Is A Witch - October Country
- Timeless - Taylor Swift
- In The Next Life - Kim Petras

contents

I'd always been taught that black cats were a sign of good luck. Maybe that just came with the territory as the daughter of a witch, but every time I'd seen one, life seemed to look up.

A flash of black caught my eye as I winded through the quiet, shady street towards town.

This one was perched on the edge of the brick wall that bordered the path, his flicking tail garnering my attention as he licked his paw, like he didn't have a care in the world.

Though I supposed he didn't. I sighed to myself. *The life of a cat.*

"If only we could all be so lucky to laze around all day like you," I said with a snort.

The little beast didn't have a collar, so I assumed he didn't have an owner. Shaking my head at myself, I adjusted the tote bag on my arm and continued on my way down the path.

Crunchy leaves littered the ground, giving a satisfying *crunch* anytime I stepped on one with my boots. The entire world was lit up with color, all the trees turning the magnificent hues of autumn.

Turning around, I looked back at the brick wall, but the cat was already gone.

I loved every bit of this season—when the air turned crisp and you could pull all the warm sweaters out of the back of your closet. It felt like the equivalent of wrapping yourself up in a warm, cozy blanket with a cup of hot apple cider in your hands.

But there was something extra special about the fall in Pleasant Grove. This town had always been a secret haven for witches, a cozy little town full of covens, where magic was *ordinary*. Long ago, the founding witches had shielded this place from the outside world, putting up protective barriers with magic. Giving us the freedom to be ourselves, not having to hide who we were.

I smiled as I saw a cobweb covered front porch; the lawn decorated with a giant spider. Families had begun putting out their Halloween decorations weeks ago. In our community, it was like a huge competition. We took it as seriously as the humans did their Christmas lights.

It was my favorite month of the year. Ever since I was small, I'd looked forward to my family attending the town's festivities together. There was nothing better than the days where we'd decorate our house for *All Hallows' Eve*, especially when there was a pot of pumpkin juice brewing.

I missed that.

The tantalizing aroma of sugar and baked goods hit me before I'd even reached for the door handle of the bakery and coffee shop in town—*The Witches' Brew*. My sister and I had opened it several years ago, and it was still crazy to me how popular we were each morning.

But right now, it was quiet, the morning dew still settled across the town as the world only just began to wake up.

The bell rang as I entered the shop, my mouth watering

from whatever was currently baking in the back. The sugar cookies were my sister's specialty, iced with such precision. Everything she made was amazing, but I eagerly awaited fall each year, knowing that it meant pumpkin-flavored treats.

Heading into the kitchen, I dropped my bag onto the chair and went to grab my apron, smoothing my light brown hair into a ponytail.

"Wil!" Luna's blonde curls popped into view. "Good morning!" Her cheery voice instantly smoothed over my unsettled mood. She'd always done that for me.

We were almost perfect mirrors of each other, my sister and I, except for our hair. We had the same little nose, the same bright green eyes, the same slant to our nose. And while she'd inherited my mom's beautiful honey-blonde hair, I'd gotten the caramel shade from our dad.

"Morning," I replied, tying the apron behind my back, inhaling deeply as if I could absorb the scent in the air. "How was your morning?"

Her dedication to the bakery side of our shop was the reason we had a line out the door most mornings. What skills I had with brewing potions, Luna had gained in her efficiency with breads, muffins, and all things sweet.

"It's been good." Luna's face split into a grin. "I made your favorite."

Mmm. I thought I had scented them in the air. "Are those chocolate chip pumpkin scones?"

"You got it." She flicked her finger, levitating one over to me.

When we were young, our parents had encouraged us not to rely on our magic. Not all witches in our town, or even in our coven, had telekinetic abilities, but we were both lucky. Our powers had gotten us out of quite a few situations in a pinch.

The scone—still warm from the oven—landed into my

hand, and I bit into it happily. "Oh. So good," I moaned. "I needed that. This morning has been, well..."

I'd barely been able to drag myself out of bed this morning. And then there was the cat. I blinked.

"I saw a cat," I said, the words slipping out.

Luna raised an eyebrow. "Babe. There are almost as many cats in Pleasant Grove as there are Witches. It's the most common familiar, after all."

Familiars were no secret in this town, and most people bonded for life with theirs. They weren't just pets—they were part of the family.

The special bond you developed went beyond just *pets* and *owners*.

I'd had that once before—with my first cat, Binx—a big fluffy gray thing. The moment they had placed him in my arms at six years old, it was like I *knew*. He understood me, down to my soul. We had a connection that couldn't be replicated. He'd been my familiar, my lifelong companion, and the creature of my heart.

But twenty-two years was a long time for any cat to live.

This summer, we'd dug a tiny grave in our backyard, Luna etching the little stone by hand.

Now my house was empty—quiet.

But it wasn't just that. "This was... different." I shrugged.

"Willow." Her voice was soft—quiet. "I know you miss Binx. But maybe it's time."

To move on.

To accept that I'd have to find a new animal to fill my heart. My potions lacked a certain luster lately. Like something was missing.

Luckily, I could still make a mean mocha, since I ran the coffee shop side of our business.

I took a deep breath. "I know."

Binx had a good life. It was time to let his soul go into the afterworld, to the beyond. He'd earned that right.

But it didn't solve my loneliness. My sister had moved out of our parent's home, the one we grew up in, six months ago, leaving me alone in the creaky old Victorian manor. I kept saying I needed to update it, but I hadn't worked up the courage to go see the twins about renovations. If we weren't witches, I would have sworn ghosts haunted it. Maybe it was.

"I was thinking about going to the shelter. Just to see."

If there was a connection. If one called out to me. I'd been avoiding going for months. What was I scared of? That none of them would bond to me—or that one would?

I sighed, shaking my head. "I just need to get out of this funk."

Luna dipped her finger in her icing bowl. "You know, it's a good thing that the Pumpkin Festival is right around the corner. And Halloween! That always cheers you up." She plopped that finger in her mouth, licking the icing off. "Needs more vanilla," she said, crinkling up her nose.

"Yeah, but..."

I didn't have a good excuse, so I just busied myself by getting the coffee ready.

My sister crossed her arms over her chest, staring at me. "Isn't Eryne working the counter today? Why don't you take the day off? Go *look*. And maybe go do something *fun*. You're acting like your soulmate died, or something."

"Hey!" I frowned. No, that aspect of my life had *long* been dead. When was the last man I'd even dated? Probably before my parent's death.

There was a reason I was twenty-eight and still single. The last few years, I'd hidden away, only leaving my parent's home for work, errands and to see my coven. I was a homebody, I'd admit. I preferred curling up on my couch with a blanket and a bowl of popcorn to going out.

"There's always The Enchanted Cauldron too," she said, a sly smile on her face. "Who knows, Mr. Perfect might just waltz in and sweep you off your broom."

I snorted. "As if."

But my brain couldn't help conjuring an image of a man—tall, dark, and handsome—swooping in to give me the most romantic night of my life. A girl could dream, right?

I shook my head. That wasn't happening. Besides, I'd tried it before. I'd sworn off men, especially human men, for a reason.

"Maybe mom was right," she mused. "When she said we should look into our futures. See who we'd end up with."

I shook my head. "You know better than to meddle in our own lives."

Some witches made a business of it. Even within our community, there were only a few blessed with the sight, putting them in high demand for their skills.

Luna didn't like to call herself a Seer, but she had strong precognition skills. Instead of opening her own fortune telling shop, or moving to the human world to offer her services there, she'd chosen to pursue her passion.

Baking.

On the other hand, I hadn't figured out my true, *genuine* passion yet. I was good at running our business, managing both sides and running the coffee shop, but it had never truly *fulfilled* me. Not like it did Luna. She was only three years younger than me, but she already seemed to have so much more figured out.

Maybe that was why I said what I did. Why I decided I'd stop living my sad little witch life, the one where I practically floated in stasis. Like my hands were holding me up, but not moving. I wanted to move—to *fly*.

To live.

"You know what... Let's do it."

Her mouth dropped open as she stared at me over the bowl of icing. "What?"

"Let's go to the bar. We deserve a night out. You can wear one of those dresses I know you have stashed in the back of your closet, just waiting for the occasion."

She squealed, throwing her arms around me. "Oh, Wil! We're going to have so much fun!"

Her eyes dragged over my outfit, from the knee length orange corduroy skirt to the black body suit I'd tucked into it, topping it off with my favorite hat. Sure, it wasn't *sexy*, but it was me. Comfortable. And the skirt had pockets.

Luna frowned. "You're not wearing that, though."

I sighed. "Promise you'll go easy on me?"

Her face lit up. Trust my sister to be the one pastel-loving witch in this town. "I know just the thing." She looked around before making a *shooing* motion with her hands. "Now go! Get out of here! I'll come over once we're all closed up."

Thankfully, running a coffee shop and bakery in a small town meant having set hours, since no one really needed anything after about 4pm. After that, there was the diner, and the bar, and we were all too happy to close up early.

"Fine, fine," I huffed, snagging another scone and levitating it over towards me. "But I'm taking this as collateral."

Luna winked before ushering me out of the kitchen. I had a few things to finish up before I could actually leave, getting things ready to open for the day. Brewing the coffee, I steamed a cup of milk, sighing in satisfaction as the smells mixed.

I might not have had everything figured out, but at least I had coffee.

If nothing else, it kept me going.

Leaving the shop, I ate one last bite of my second scone, sipping on the coffee I'd made myself before Eryne had arrived. She was my favorite hire of the last year, down from her redheaded bob to the cute witchy earrings she wore to work every day. It was hard not to be festive when you worked in a store like The Witches' Brew. Today's were a pair of brooms.

It wasn't even seven am yet. The morning was still young. I supposed I could go to the library, or maybe pop into my favorite apothecary shop. No doubt my reserves on herbs and supplies were running low at home, though I had plenty of time to restock before the next coven night.

I could go to the pet shop, but... I didn't know if I was ready yet. It might have been months, but I still felt like I needed time.

Rubbing at the back of my neck, I sat on a bench on main street, taking in a deep drink of my pumpkin spice latte. This spot gave me the perfect view of our town, Main Street just beginning to come alive as people began to scurry about town, heading to their jobs and lives. Most of the shops didn't open until nine, so even though the roads were busy, the sidewalks were still quiet.

It was the perfect way to enjoy the morning. Pulling a book out of my tote bag, I opened to the page I'd left off, letting the silence of the morning draw me into the world.

There was nothing quite as magical as getting lost in the pages of a good book. I'd always loved that feeling—looking up, and realizing I'd just spent the last three straight hours reading without a break.

When I finally put my bookmark back in, I checked the time. I'd agreed to meet Luna tonight, but what did I do with my free day? Sure, I'd done my job this morning—prep, but I didn't need to balance the books. I'd already placed the orders for the next two weeks.

That meant... I really was free to do whatever I wanted.

Should I go to the pet shelter like Luna suggested?

I thought about the black cat from this morning, the one with no collar around his neck. No home. Was there a cat there, as lonely and desperate for companionship as I was?

That was what made me pause—the idea that someone else out there needed me too.

I shoved my book back into my bag, turning to go the other way on Main Street.

Towards the animal shelter.

"If you see anyone who you feel a connection with, or just want to take a closer look at, just call me over. I'm happy to let you visit with them, so you can see if you have a bond." The young witch gave me a smile before leaving me in the room of cages.

It was hard to describe how deep the bond went between a witch and her familiar, but it was the reason I hadn't been ready to replace Binx yet.

But... It was time. I knew it.

I wanted someone to come home to.

Even if that someone was, well... my cat.

Staring at the cages, I walked back and forth. The sweet brown cat stretched out her back, but despite the adorable twitch to her nose, I felt... nothing. Same with the tabby in the kennel next to her, and every one after that. Dozens of cats passed by, and there was no tug, no pull. No connection.

And yet... the black cat in front of me flicked his tail. Locked his bright yellow eyes onto mine, and then licked his paw.

He looked just like the cat from this morning. But that was impossible, wasn't it?

Even familiars weren't actually *magic*.

Lucifer, his little name tag read. He looked like a young cat, though certainly nothing like the little kitten I'd gotten all those years ago. There was something about him, though. Something that screamed, *'Take me home. I'm yours.'*

That was the bond I'd been looking for. He tilted his head at me and blinked.

Who was I to argue with destiny? Hopefully, we would have many years together.

"Excuse me?" I asked the girl working at the shelter. "Can I... hold him?" I gestured to his cage.

Gods, I wanted to get him out of here. He seemed almost... irritated to be stuck in this over glorified glass box.

He deserved a big house to run around where he could chase mice and be petted to his heart's content. And I could give him that. The biggest perk of inheriting the Clarke manor was I had plenty of space for the little beastie.

"Oh, him?" She asked me, wrinkling her nose. "He's not very friendly. Are you sure?"

I nodded my head. "Yes, please."

She shrugged, bringing me into a back room before she returned with the cat.

My cat.

Once the worker left, he padded over to me almost tentatively, cocking his head in an un-catlike manner as he watched me.

Another flick of his tail.

"Hey, kitty," I cooed, holding out a hand towards him as he sat in front of me.

I tilted my head to the side, staring at him. "What's your name, hm?"

The cat seemed to snort, as if the name the humans had given him annoyed him. He didn't look like a Lucifer, even though when the light hit his eyes in a certain way they appeared almost... *red.*

But that couldn't be possible.

I held out my hand, and he brushed against it. "They said you're not friendly, but you're like a little sweetheart, aren't you?" I cooed.

And then he nudged my hand with his head, letting me pet him as he rubbed all over me, before climbing into my lap and laying down.

The purring all but confirmed that this was the one.

"Want to come home with me, huh, little beastie?" I scratched the top of his head.

He meowed, looking up at me.

"I'll take that as a yes."

Scooping him up in my arms, I knocked on the door, summoning back the witch.

"I'll take him," I said, giving an affirmative nod. And if in agreement, the cat cuddled lazily into my arms, not a care in the world to me holding him.

Even my sister's cat didn't let me hold her.

The young witch peered at me skeptically. "You want the demon cat?"

I held him against my chest, frowning. "Yes. And he's not a demon." I scratched between his ears, and he looked up at me. "Are you, beastie?"

If only I had known.

11

T he collar jingled around my neck that the damned humans had snapped on me.

Didn't they know I wasn't a cat?

I mean, I looked like a cat in my current form, *sure*.

But that was because I was stuck like this. It certainly wasn't by choice. All thanks to one *godsforsaken* night.

A month. I'd been stuck in this shape for a month, and what did I have to show for it? A collar and practically permanent residency at this shelter.

I didn't belong in a shelter, for crying out loud. Sure, I could escape, but that didn't solve my current predicament.

If only I had my magic, I'd have figured a way out of this mess.

But no. They had confined me to a cage, which forced me to stare at my reflection, wishing I could get out of this damn form. To make matters worse, they'd given me a name. And not one that was benefiting of my caliber. *No.*

I preferred when they called me *Demon Cat* to anything else. At least that one was accurate.

But this human... I'd sensed her.

Something about her scent drew me towards her, and I hadn't even needed to suppress the cat-like urges that grew stronger by the day.

She'd looked into my eyes, and a part of me knew I could trust her.

And maybe... she could help me.

That was why I'd practically crawled into her lap. Why I let her take me.

"What do you think?" The human mumbled, carrying me into her house. "I know it's not in the best of shape, but... it's home."

The outside of the old Victorian mansion was just like I would have imagined it, down to the broom that rested against the siding.

And the inside was *warm*. It was clearly a home. A family's home.

But where was her family? The human didn't seem to have anyone else living with her, and I didn't detect the traces of anyone else. Maybe a faint smell of another human—female, and then some older ones, but nothing else.

It's nice. I thought. *Better than any home I've ever had.* But I couldn't say that.

She'd carried me into the kitchen, setting me onto the floor as she rustled through the fridge, clearly frowning at its contents.

"What do you think, little beastie? Do you want some water? I need to go to the store to get some things..." She bit her lip. "I didn't exactly expect this to happen today." She sighed, her cheeks turning slightly pink as she continued mumbling to herself.

Oh. That was cute.

I cocked my head, staring at her with fervent attention as she filled a bowl with water.

She stopped, staring back at me. "Will you be okay while I go?"

Crouching down to place the water bowl on the floor, she rubbed between my ears, and an involuntary *purr* emitted from my throat.

That was... new.

I'd never really had the occasion to let humans pet me when I was in this form before. It surprised me how much I liked it when *she* did it.

I meowed in response. I hoped that it communicated, *I'll be fine, human.*

But what did I know?

The human stood up, brushing off her orange skirt—cat hair I'd left behind, I was sure—and then nodded at me.

"Okay, boy. I'll be back. Be good and don't get into anything." She winced, looking around the room. "I'll have to clean up when I get back. Geez."

I flicked my ears back in amusement as the human talked to herself.

"Gods, Willow," she muttered to herself. *Willow.* I liked that. "You have got to stop talking to the cat like he's going to respond."

If only she knew.

Heading to the door, the human—Willow, I corrected myself—picked up her phone, hitting a contact before putting it to her ear.

"Yeah, Luna?" she said into the speaker. "I'm going to need a raincheck for tonight..." She winced. "I know. I'm sorry—" And then she was out the door, leaving me all alone to explore my new home.

Flicking my tail, I walked across the human's hardwood floors. I figured if I was stuck here till I figured out how to reverse this damned curse, I might as well get my lay of the land.

What's this? My nose caught a scent and I couldn't help but follow it.

What was that delicious scent? My mouth watered, and I knew it was the feline side of me that had been dominant for too long. That was what guided me through the rooms of the house, searching for the location of the wafting smell.

Pushing open the cracked door, I padded into a room, stopping suddenly as all of my senses were overwhelmed by *her*. Willow. Her scent was all over this room, and I realized with a jolt exactly where I'd entered a moment later. Bedroom.

Darting out of the room, I dashed to the other end of the house—peeking my head into what looked like a library. There was an empty bedroom with lilac walls, and then—there was the source of the twitching to my nose.

It smelled like catnip, rosemary, marigolds—the things my cat side *loved*.

The room itself seemed to be some large storage room, though everything had its place. The back wall was covered in bookshelves, filled with a whole myriad of supplies: essential oils, crystals, plants, herbs, dried flowers, candles, incense and books.

Jumping on the table in the center, I surveyed the crystal ball, a grimoire laying open, plus a stack of books, and more candles that littered the table.

It suddenly occurred to me what exactly she used this room for.

Witch.

And then a thought ran through my mind.

This female—she could *fix* me. She could end this damned curse and turn me back into my proper form.

Maybe luck was on my side when they brought me to the animal shelter here. I'd certainly never have expected to end up in a town with a coven of witches.

Fates.

I needed this undone.

But how...?

She was back, with a bag of cat toys and treats at her side.

"Here, kitty," the brunette girl cooed, shaking a bag of treats. I sat on the floor in front of her as she held the bag.

Internally, I rolled my eyes, flicking my tail to show my irritation.

"Come on," she said, sighing. "They're good. At least, I think." Willow looked in the bag, as if questioning it now.

Sniffing it, I scrunched up my nose. It was bad enough that I'd had to eat whatever the shelter gave me for the last few weeks. I'd barely survived on the scraps except for when I dared to sneak out.

But this? *No.* I couldn't bring myself so low.

I wasn't a cat, dammit.

Willow frowned. "Do you not like treats?" The expression gave her worry lines on her brows, and I instantly wanted to smooth them out.

Why, Damien? Why was that the thought that had popped into my mind?

I jumped to my feet, padding over in search of *real* food. Something palatable that I'd actually be able to stomach. Not dry kibble or whatever they put in those cat treats everyone tried to feed me.

"Where are you going, little beastie?" The witch murmured, following me as I sauntered through the living room into the kitchen.

Planting myself in front of the fridge, I meowed.

Opening the doors, she looked at the contents. "What do you want, hm? Tuna?" She pulled out a can.

I flicked my ears back in disgust. *No, thank you.* I'd never been a huge fan.

"Hmm." She diverted her attention back to the drawer, bringing out a fresh cut of salmon. "What about this?"

Meow. I brushed up against her legs in approval.

She chuckled to herself. "Picky cat, huh?"

My little witch had no idea.

Willow sighed. "Guess I'm making you dinner, then. I don't think raw salmon is good for cats."

I gave her a chirp of confirmation before curling up in the corner, letting my head rest on my front paws as I watched her cook. She was a natural in the kitchen, which made me wonder about the potions room I'd seen. Despite how easy it would be for disarray, the entire room was meticulous, organized—like everything had its place.

I had a feeling she was equally skilled with whatever concoction she was brewing.

And now I had to brew my plan—one to get her to help me.

How not to startle her when I revealed my true identity.

There was something nagging in my gut—*what was it?* The feeling settled within me, though I couldn't identify it.

"Here you go, beastie," she said, placing a plate at my paws.

My nose twitched as she stared at me, her eyes darting

between the cooked salmon and me. *Are you going to watch me eat, little witch?*

Apparently she was. I sniffed the cooked fish, and after deeming it smelled good—she'd grilled it perfectly. I took a bite.

Oh, Hell. I gobbled up the entire piece of fish, tearing through the entire fillet faster than I could blink.

Willow scratched under my chin. "You *were* hungry. Poor little guy, huh? I still have to figure out what to call you."

Demon Cat is fine, I thought, sitting up to stare at her.

She snorted, not breaking eye contact. "I still can't believe they called you a demon cat. You're such a sweet little boy, aren't you?" My witch scratched under my chin, and I let out an involuntary purr.

Damien, I thought, hoping whatever bond she seemed to feel between us would communicate that. *My name is Damien.*

I'd never willingly given my name to a human before, but... I didn't think I minded her knowing it.

Didn't mind being here, even if they'd trapped me in this feline body.

Willow's lips tilted up into a smile. "Damien?"

Yes! I meowed excitedly, brushing back and forth against her legs, nuzzling my head against her skin.

"Damien. I like it, too." She scooped me up into her arms, cradling me like a baby. "What do you say we go sit on the couch and watch a movie, huh, beastie? There's so many good ones for the Halloween season."

Meow.

Yes.

Domesticity was never a part of my life before. I'd never really had the chance to just sit and *be.* There had always been something else for me to do, something my brother needed from me. I was never my own person.

But maybe here, in this town, at this witch's house, everything would be different.

So I let her carry me to the couch. Curled up on her lap, and watched a couple fall in love while they rebuilt an old bed-and-breakfast. Snorted when they were clearly too stupid to admit their own feelings. Watched with rapt attention, until the warmth of the little witch's lap lulled me to sleep. I'd never felt so comforted, so at peace.

Maybe life as a cat wasn't so bad. That was the thought that startled me awake.

I couldn't afford to think like this. I didn't know what was wrong with me, but I had to get out of this body—before the change was permanent. If there was even a chance I had to remain as a cat forever, I needed to do everything I could to fix it.

Willow stood up and yawned, stretching out her arms before turning back to me.

I tried to push the nagging feeling aside and remind myself that it could wait until tomorrow.

Curiously, I angled my head and perked my ear up towards her. Did she expect me to sleep in her room? That felt like a line I shouldn't cross. Especially considering I wasn't *actually* a cat.

And I'd have to break the news to her, eventually. That I wouldn't *be* her cat. That I wasn't a cat at all.

But when she looked at me, tucking her hair behind her ear as I peered at her from the couch, I could sense how vulnerable she was. How alone this little witch was.

And I didn't want her to feel like that.

"Should we go to bed now, Damien?"

Meow. I got up, stretching my back, and hopped off the couch, following her loyally.

Witch's best friend, I thought with a smirk.

Despite my upbringing not to consort with witches, this

woman had done everything she could to make me happy. Comfortable.

Even if I was just her cat.

I curled up at the witch's feet, and for the first night in weeks, I slept.

G ood morning, beastie," I murmured to the black
ball of fur, who was currently sitting up, licking his
front paws as he lounged on my bed.

I'd put on my orange buffalo plaid comforter when I'd
decorated the house inside for fall, and he almost looked like
the perfect little stuffed animal laying on it. Especially when
my decorative pumpkin pillow was against the pillow shams.

Meow. It was crazy to me how even though he was a fairly
quiet cat, I almost felt like I could tell what he was thinking.
What he was *saying*, even with a simple meow. *Good morning,
human.*

I'd slept better than I had in weeks last night. Was it
because I'd known there was another being in the house? This
old, creaky house could get lonely.

"I have to work today," I said, petting him slowly. "But I
won't be gone all day—just for the morning rush—because
Luna, my sister, she'll need me. I don't enjoy leaving her alone,
you know?"

He chirped in agreement.

"I feel bad leaving you alone too, little beastie. But I'll pick up more salmon on the way home, and then maybe we can watch another movie? Snuggle on the couch?"

Why was I narrating my entire day to the cat I'd just adopted yesterday? I couldn't explain it, but the way he looked up at me with those gigantic eyes told me he understood, too.

Damien brushed up against my hand. Instantly, the contact centered me. Calmed me down. I'd never felt anything that gave me such an immediate sense of rightness, but I guessed that was a sign of good synastry between us.

I sighed. *Time to get going.* I didn't want to leave my warm, cozy bed. Damien was basically a bed warmer with his cozy warmth keeping my feet nice and toasty.

Picking him up, I scratched under his chin before nuzzling at his face. "Who's a cute little boy, huh?" He squirmed as I rubbed my nose against his cheek.

I laughed as he jumped out of my arms, moving to the other side of the bed to lick his paws.

Rejected from any further love, I finally forced myself out of bed. Shucking my shirt off, I whisked it into my dirty clothes hamper, the rest of my clothes following behind, and I headed to the bathroom.

Maybe after I'd had a solid few hours of work in the bakery, this strange feeling in my gut would go away.

I could only hope.

Luna's hands were kneading a ball of cookie dough when I came into the kitchen area, unwrapping my scarf from around my neck and hanging it up on a hook.

"How was your night?" She narrowed her eyes on me.

I winced. "I'm sorry for canceling our plans. It's just... I took your advice."

"Looking into your future?" Luna perked up.

"No." Snorting, I went to pull my hair back so I could help her with prep. "I went to the shelter."

"Oh. And?"

"And... I got a cat."

She blinked. "That soon?"

"Uh-huh." I whipped around from the fridge, where I'd been grabbing the heavy cream to make some fresh whipped toppings for drinks. "What do you mean, *that soon?* You're the one who told me to *go.*"

"Yeah, but I figured you'd avoid it for another few months. That's what you always do."

Always? I cleared my throat, dropping my eyes to the floor. "I do not."

Luna's voice grew quiet. "Willow. You don't have to pretend with me. I know you didn't pick this, either." She indicated around us at the shop.

"But I love—"

"I know." She shook her head. "But that doesn't change the way you've always avoided decisions: What to do after college? Selling mom and dad's house? Building your own life?" She smiled sadly at me.

"I..." But I couldn't exactly deny most of it. "I'm not selling the house." Crossing my arms over my chest, I frowned. "There's no reason to. I told you that. It's my house now." Our house, until she'd chosen to move out.

When did my little sister get so introspective?

"There are other houses," she mumbled.

"I don't want other houses, Lu. We've gone over this."

"I just worry about you, all alone in that creaky old house."

"So move back in." I shrugged, like we hadn't had this

discussion multiple times since she'd brought up moving out and into the studio apartment above the bakery. "Besides, I'm not alone now. I have Damien."

"Damien?" She raised an eyebrow.

"*My cat.*"

"Right."

"Luna..."

She shook her head, her bandana that was holding her hair back swishing with the movement. "I'm sorry. I overstepped."

"No. You're right." Luna's eyes shot to mine, the surprise as clear in her eyes as I figured it was on my face. "I need to figure out my life. What I want. If..." I didn't want to say it. I loved working with my sister. "If this is it." Maybe it wasn't?

She nodded. "It's okay, you know. To make your own decisions. Even if it's not this."

I dumped the heavy cream into the blender, along with the flavoring, busying myself so I didn't have to meet her eyes again.

All morning, I pondered that very thought.

Because it felt like there was something out there waiting for me, and I didn't know what it was yet.

But I wanted to find out.

The entire morning and afternoon passed by in a blur. Saturdays during October were always a hustle and bustle of activity. The crisp autumn air was filled with the sounds of laughter and chatter as most of the town was out enjoying the perfect fall weather. Practically everyone in town had made a pit stop for Luna's famous pumpkin cookies.

I couldn't blame them. I'd snuck three over the course of the day.

Early afternoon, I took off, leaving Luna to close up. I never considered myself a morning person, but I loved getting off early. It was the one perk of going in before the sun rose.

And now, I was probably wearing my footprints into the kitchen floor, walking back and forth as I nibbled on another cookie. Luna's words from earlier were still bouncing around my mind.

Was I always avoiding making the big decisions? Waiting for someone else to make them for me?

Damien was sitting on top of my kitchen table, staring at me, but I didn't have the mental energy to make him get down.

"Are you going to pace like that all day?"

I blinked.

Stared at the black cat as he flicked his tail.

"What? You've never seen a talking cat before?"

"Willow, you're losing your mind," I muttered to myself. "That cat is not talking to you."

"No, I am." He jumped off the table, coming to sit at my feet. "But I'm not *technically* a cat." He tilted his head to the side, those ears pointing up adorably.

I raised my eyebrow. "You have whiskers. And a *tail.*"

And now I'm talking to my cat.

"Well, I'm certainly aware that I *look* like a cat." He licked one of his paws. "But I'm not. I'm just stuck."

"Stuck?" *Did he just narrow his cat-eyes at me?*

I'm going crazy. That was the only logical answer to this. I'd lost it.

"Yes. I can't shift back to my normal form."

"And your normal form is?"

"A man. Mostly."

"*Mostly?* What the hell does that mean?"

"I'm not sure you're ready for that." His eyes flickered red, and I could have sworn the room darkened.

Oh. "Well..." I bit my lip. "How do we get you, um... de-catted? *De-catified?*" I pondered the term, and then shook my head. "Has this happened before?"

"No." He heaved a dramatic sigh. "I was cursed. By a witch."

Oh my gods. "A cursed talking cat? What is this, *Sabrina the Teenage Witch?*"

He blinked his eyes at me. "What?"

"You know... Salem? He's cursed to be a..." I looked at his blank face. Clearly, he'd never watched human television. "Never mind." I crossed my arms over my chest. "How do we fix it?"

"Hmm?" His voice came out scratchy, almost a purr. Which made sense. Since I was talking to a *cat*.

My legs wobbled, and I lowered myself to the ground, sitting on the hardwood floor. I wasn't sure I could keep myself upright if I stayed standing. Not with the events currently unfolding in front of me.

I blinked. What was the proper response in this situation? I'd never dealt with a person-turned-cat before. Of all the weird magical things that had happened in Pleasant Grove, this topped the list.

"How do we turn you back to your proper form, then?"

"Now, now, little witch." His little pink nose wiggled. "What's so wrong with our little arrangement?"

My nostrils flared. "Our little *arrangement?* You mean the one where you bamboozled your way into my home, got me to feed you, and slept on my bed? That one?"

He licked his paw nonchalantly. "Yes."

"Oh my—" *Goddess be.*

Slept on my bed.

"Did you see me naked?"

Damien the cat froze. "What?"

"This morning. When I changed. You were in my room, and I—" I paled, glad I was sitting on the ground. "I'm going to be sick."

"Little witch." He placed a paw on my arm. "I promise, I did not look." *Much*, the little grin on his face seemed to say.

I rolled my eyes. "Willow."

"What?"

"My name. It's Willow."

He flicked his tail. "I know."

"Then why do you keep calling me *little witch*?" I was five-six, a perfectly average height, thank you very much.

"Well, you are, aren't you? A witch?" Damien tilted his head to the side. "Which is why you can help."

I crossed my arms over my chest. "Sure, but I'm not *little*. I'm twenty-eight, and I'm a business owner. Even this house is mine."

"You called me your *little baby boy* three times this morning."

I cleared my throat. "I thought you were a cat."

"As normal people do." He purred.

"*Damien.*" It felt weird addressing him like that—with his name. When it had popped into my head, I'd thought nothing of it, but now—

"Ah, see, you already know my name, *witch.*" His nose twitched.

Goddess help me. You've truly lost your marbles, Willow.

"You're not insane."

"What? Did you just read my mind?" I rubbed at my temples.

"No. I can't access my full powers in this form, unfortunately."

27

"Full powers?" I raised an eyebrow.

Damien stretched his back before sitting up, like he was drawing up his full cat-height. His eyes flickered red again, and I shivered, even though there wasn't normally a draft in here.

"What are you...?" The words came out barely above a whisper.

His black tail flicked against the floor. "I'm sorry I didn't properly introduce myself before. I didn't want to startle you."

Well, you did a pretty good job of that, anyway.

"My name *is* Damien, though I suppose Demon Cat is also appropriate." His ear twitched. I didn't think I was imagining the chuckle in his voice. "I'm the bastard prince of the Demon King, and that makes me—"

"A demon." I paled. My mom had always warned me about demons and their trickster ways. How they'd steal your soul and condemn you to an eternity in their realm. Hell.

Which meant this cat—my cat—was from *hell.*

'And never, ever, make a deal with the devil.' She'd always warned me of that, ever since I was a little girl. I sucked in a breath. I had a feeling I'd done something a lot worse by inviting this being into my home.

"You look like you're finally getting it now," Damien the *demon*—the cat, currently sitting next to me—said. "Now, can we get back to the important part?"

I ignored his question, still reeling in my surprise. "How did this happen to you if you're the *son* of the *Demon King*? Aren't you like... *super* powerful?" What little I knew about demons wasn't helping me here.

He narrowed his eyes, and the temperature dropped a few more degrees. "Say that again when I'm not in this form, and you'll see just how powerful I am."

But this black cat glaring at me with red eyes made me burst out laughing. "I'm sorry. I just can't take you seriously.

You're so *cute.*" I *booped* his nose in demonstration, watching as he wiggled his whiskers.

"Willow." His eyes narrowed into slits. "I'm serious."

"So—" I couldn't stop giggling. "—am I."

He climbed up, putting one paw in the center of my chest so he could put the other one over my mouth.

"Listen to me, little witch. I need your help to reverse this damn curse so I can go back to my proper form. My *life.*"

I moved his paw off my face, dangling his cat-self out in front of me. "And you expect me to do this out of the goodness of my heart?"

"Well, a little, yes. But also... You *have* heard of making a deal with a demon, haven't you?"

I narrowed my eyes. "Enough to know I shouldn't make one."

Damien sighed, flicking his tail again in annoyance. "I can give you anything you want in return for helping me. Whatever your heart desires."

"But I—" I blinked. There wasn't anything I needed, but what *did* my heart desire? It was something I'd been thinking about. Not that I was going to tell him that.

"Everybody wants something, Willow." He licked his paw. "Even good little witches like you."

Ignoring his comment, and how it made me feel, I frowned. "So, how do I turn you back? Is it some spell, or potion I need to make, or..."

His eyes focused on mine. Unblinking. "I don't know. If I did, don't you think I would have undone it myself by now?"

Oh. Well. I guessed that would make sense.

"Yeah." I muttered under my breath. "But I have little experience with curses. None of the witches here would ever use them. They're banned in the community. Our coven hardly even discusses them, even though I think Cait would love to hex her ex-boyfriend for good measure. Although..."

My thoughts wandered to the library my parents had spent years amassing. I'd read so many of them, but maybe there was something in there that would tell me how I could break this curse.

"Maybe I have an idea."

I didn't need anything from him, but the sooner I could get him out of my house, out of my life, the better. Because Demons were not to be trifled with.

damien

"Do normal people take their familiars to the library?" I asked Willow, following behind her as we walked the path to town.

I could have teleported us if I'd had full use of my magic. But then again, if I'd had full use of my magic, I wouldn't have been here, walking behind the witch.

"No."

Somehow, that wasn't as annoying as it had been before. Especially now that I could actually talk to Willow. I had startled her yesterday, but she seemed to have gotten used to me talking now.

I'd been on this path before, but everything felt new walking beside her. The little bell on my collar jingled when I moved, something I'd been steadily ignoring for weeks.

"So... How exactly did you end up stuck as a cat?"

"I told you. A witch cursed me."

"Mhm." She bit her lip, a motion I'd noticed she seemed to do often when she was deep in thought. "And what did you do, exactly?"

"Who said I did anything?" I walked faster in front of her

so I could jump up onto a short wall, sitting on it and staring at her.

Willow rolled her eyes, continuing to walk down the path. "No witch would curse an innocent man."

"But I'm not a man, remember?"

It was her turn to come to a screeching halt. "Are you telling me someone found out you were a demon and then did this to you?" Her eyes looked almost... concerned. I didn't deserve that.

"Something like that." I couldn't explain to her *why* I was in the human realm, why I'd been out where a witch could curse me in the first place, but when you boiled it down, that was what happened.

"And no one's come looking for you? No one's... worried about you?" Her eyes were glassy. And how strange was that? That this little witch was concerned for me?

I shook my head. No one would come looking. My half-brother wouldn't give a second thought to my absence as long as I completed my task.

"Come on," Willow said, scooping me up into her arms. Cuddling me like she had before work yesterday, even though she knew what I was now. "Library is just around the corner."

"Why are you carrying me, little witch?" I muttered, tilting my head up to look at her. "I can walk just fine."

"Shush, beastie. I don't want them to think I've gone completely nuts."

She scratched my head, and I let out an involuntary satisfied meow in response before settling into the hold.

I... didn't hate it. Maybe it was because it was her? I had razor-sharp claws in this form, and yet I was perfectly content letting her carry me into the library, nuzzling my face into the crook of her elbow.

I didn't perk my head up again until the smell of old books

entered through my nostrils. The library was dark, densely filled with books. It almost felt like there was an other-worldly presence in here. I wondered how many witches had studied here, learned magic here.

"Willow!" A young man's voice called out, and I felt the hair stand up on my back.

For whatever reason, I didn't like other humans talking to my witch. *Huh.*

"Oh, hi, Simon," Willow said, the warmth clear in her tone. I didn't need to look at her to know a smile curled over her face.

"Who's this?" The redheaded boy—who could have been no older than his early twenties—pushed up the glasses onto the bridge of his nose, looking at me.

I hissed, bearing my teeth at him.

"This is my new cat. I couldn't leave him home," she said, wincing. It surprised me at how easily the lie slipped from her lips.

Though maybe she didn't trust me. I would understand why.

"I see." Simon's lips spread into a fine line as he looked at me, before turning his attention back to my human. "Is there anything you need help with today?"

"No. Just doing some research." She looked down at me, and I chirped, the sound passing through my lips unintentionally. "I promise he'll be on his best behavior."

I meowed in response, narrowing my eyes. *Yeah, as long as you don't keep looking at her like that,* young wizard.

"Damien," she huffed, her voice low as we headed towards a table in the back. "You're going to get me in trouble."

Rows of books surrounded us on either side, keeping us out of eyeshot from the other patrons. And, hopefully, out of hearing range too.

I jumped out of her arms, landing in front of the table. "I didn't like how he was looking at you."

Willow deposited her bag onto a seat, draping her coat over the back. "He's my *friend*. I've known him since I was a toddler. Goddess help me." She rubbed at her temples. "Now, you stay here. I'm going to go see what I can find on curses."

"You don't want me to come?"

I found I didn't like that, either. I wanted to stay by her side. Protect her. Even if I weighed ten pounds, I still had sharp claws. And pointy teeth.

If anyone threatened her...

"You don't think it's going to look weird if I wander around the library *talking to my cat*?"

"Mm. Point taken." Laying down, I curled my body up into a ball, resting my head on my paws so I could still watch her.

"Don't hiss at anyone else," she warned me before taking off in a blur of orange and brown. The hit of her sweet scent— like coffee and vanilla and something *else*—caught my nose.

There was something satisfying about that, just watching her. Every so often, she'd disappear from my line of sight, and then she'd return to our table, depositing another handful of books. I stayed quiet, just a few meows of acknowledgment. I couldn't help but notice how her face lit up when she brushed her hand over my back, and the way her eyes sparkled when she rubbed that spot in between my ears.

I already hated the thought of leaving her. It was strange, the affection I felt for this human. This little witch. Despite having just met her, there was already a sense of familiarity and ease.

And not just because she was so delicate with me, even though she knew now that I wasn't actually a cat.

Willow sat down with another pile in her hands and I perked up. "Anything good?"

"Shhh." She looked around, her eyes widening before turning back to the book. "Don't talk to me. It's bad enough that I brought my cat to the library."

"Not a cat."

She reached over and scratched under my chin, that involuntary purr coming from my chest. Like she was proving to me I was exactly that. I'd been stuck in this form for too long.

I narrowed my eyes. "Don't do that."

"Then let me *focus.*" Willow turned back to her pile of books, grabbing a new one out. "I'm trying to help you, after all."

Although I hated to admit it, she was right, and I sat there and watched her work while wishing I could be more useful. I lacked any real understanding of how witchcraft functioned beyond what I learned in the demon realm. Crystals, herbs, candles, potions—that much I knew. Not how their magic worked. Not the things that might actually make a difference here.

"Did you find something?" I asked, peeking over at the book she'd buried her nose into.

She shook her head. "I don't know yet." Looking down at my paws, she sighed. "I'd ask you to help, but..."

"No opposable thumbs," I agreed. "It's probably the worst part of being stuck in this form for the last month. That and being stuck in the shelter with only that horrible kibble for food." I scrunched up my nose, making a disgusted face. I hated that stuff.

She froze. "What?"

I cocked my head to the side.

"A month? You..." Her eyes grew wide. "Gods. Fuck. That's... awful. I'm sorry."

Doing my best cat-equivalent of a shrug, I curled back up on the desk, watching her read a book labeled *The Little Book of*

Curses and Maledictions for Everyday Use. She'd already set *Witchcraft: Hexes and Curses* and *Magic Spells To Curse Your Enemies* to the side. There was a pile of books in her discard pile, too, with similar names, that she must have deemed useless, barely taking the time to flick through them.

Something about the names made me want to chuckle. The titles were so on the nose. What else did I expect from a town of witches?

It could have been worse, I reminded myself, *if she hadn't rescued me.*

Because at least now I had a chance. My few experimentations with my magic in the shelter hadn't proved fruitful—except for finding Willow.

Is this better? I said into her mind.

She jolted upright. "How did you—" Willow blinked. "Did you just say something?"

Yes. I kept my eyes focused on her, watching as her green eyes grew rounder.

"But... your lips didn't move." Her voice was a hushed whisper as she leaned down closer to my fuzzy body. "Can you hear what I'm thinking, too?"

I snorted. *No.*

She looked relieved that I couldn't hear into her thoughts, and I wondered what she was hiding underneath her warm smile. What thoughts were so private that she wanted to keep them only to herself?

Besides, the only demons that had that ability were ones who had found their mates. That mind-link between a bonded pair. I wasn't one of the lucky ones who had.

"The problem is," she declared, slamming her book shut, "that I don't know what curse was placed on you. And that's crucial to the undoing of it. Which means..."

Willow took a deep breath. Stood up and paced around the

table, deep in thought. The muttering under her breath only intensified as she seemed to work through whatever problem she was having.

"Unless I... No." She pinched in between her brows. "I'm going to have to brute force it. If I untangle the threads..."

You... What? How?

"You really don't know a lot about witches, do you?"

Probably as much as you know about demons, I thought sarcastically.

"Fair point." She sighed. "A lot of these books say the same things. There are a few different methods we could try. But I don't think you're going to like them."

Try me. I'd do just about anything to get out of this form. To stretch my actual legs again.

She flipped back open a book, pointing at the passage on the page. "*Simple Curse Breaking Spells,*" Willow read off. "One. Let a source of living water carry it away." She raised an eyebrow, and I shook my head.

"I'd rather not."

"Two. Take a purifying bath with a blend of salt and—"

"I think it's safe to say anything involving water will also involve my claws." I hissed out, retracting them as if in demonstration. "The longer I stay in this form, the more catlike my reflexes become. It's... involuntary."

Willow nodded. "I can try this spell, but for best success, I would need to know who cursed you. Then I could bind them and stop the curse at its source."

"Is it dangerous?"

"What?"

"Going after the witch who cursed me."

What if you get hurt? I didn't like the idea of her risking herself for me.

"I—" Willow's cheeks pinked. "Well, I'd be okay. I can handle myself."

Oh. I hadn't realized I'd projected that last thought into her mind.

She cleared her throat. "Besides, I don't have to find her necessarily, just... know her presence? Even if you just show me your memory, I think that would help."

I hesitated. If she saw the memory, she'd know too much.

The witch who'd cursed me... Fuck. She'd been a seer. I was looking for a powerful one, and yet... I'd almost fucked everything up.

I was just lucky the curse she'd cast on me hadn't *fully* worked. If I'd fully become a cat, losing all access to myself and my powers, I would have lost my mind. I would have been stuck in this form for all of eternity.

"So let's try the spell. What do we need?" I'd do anything to keep her away from that memory.

She scanned the list. "I think I have almost everything—except a belonging of yours. And some black salt. But we need to do it on the full moon, too."

"When's the full moon?"

Willow gulped. "Tomorrow."

Which meant if it failed—I could be stuck as a cat for a whole extra month. Still, it was worth it.

"Let's do it."

My little witch nodded, scooping up the few books she'd selected into her arms. "Let me just check these out with Simon, and then we'll run into town to get the other things for the spell. Do you think you could get something of yours?"

I paused. Something of mine? I barely had anything to my name. Was anything truly *mine*? Not my title, nor my position. Even the clothes on my back weren't my own.

But there was something. I just had to go get it. "Leave it to me, little witch."

She gave me a sad smile, and I instantly wanted to make it better. To soothe her fears.

I couldn't do that as a cat. Couldn't take her beautiful face into my hands and promise her everything would be okay, not yet.

But after she fixed me, I could.

And that was the thought that sent me scurrying in search of the only thing that belonged to me. Something no one else had a claim on.

Something I'd hoped to one day need, but not for this.

He'd spent the night sleeping at my feet again, and even though I knew now that he wasn't really a cat, the action still comforted me. It was a small thing, really, to know I wasn't alone, but it made me feel better.

Damien had disappeared during the afternoon, leaving me to work in the study, making sure I had just the right balance of herbs and ingredients for the spell. It was a relatively simple task, but it still required my undivided attention.

He returned, holding something in between his teeth. After hopping up on the table, he unceremoniously dropped it onto the workstation in front of me.

"This is it?" I asked, holding up a small silver ring, the purple amethyst sparkling in the light. The setting was gorgeous—the entire piece was, really.

He cleared his throat. "It was my mother's. It's the only thing I could think of. She gave it to me before she passed away."

So he'd lost a parent, too. I knew firsthand how heartbreaking that was, and I wondered who had been by his side. Who'd helped him through the grief? How long had it been?

"I'm sorry," I whispered, brushing my finger over the stone.

Damien's big yellow cat eyes connected with mine, and I wondered what he would look like if we were successful. What color his eyes would be. If his hair was as dark as his fur. Would he have a strong jaw? His voice was deep, and I imagined—

"Little witch," he murmured, breaking me from my trance. "Shall we prepare?"

"Right." I nodded, setting the ring back down. "We still have a few hours till the sun goes down. I want to have everything ready so I can perform the spell when the moon is at its highest. That way, it's the most powerful moon magic possible. And hopefully..." I snapped my fingers.

"What are these?" Damien said, nudging a bundle of herbs with his nose.

I looked at my chosen selection. We'd talked about doing the spell, but in reality, I was trying *everything*.

"I'm going to burn it," I explained. I'd burn incense—a blend of rue, hyssop, salt, sage, and frankincense. "The smoke should hopefully help to cleanse away the curse from your body."

If it worked. Some of the herbs served specific purposes: hyssop was good for magical self-defense, while frankincense was used to cleanse and purify. Both of them would take part in my spell.

I explained all of that as I worked. Whenever he had a question, that little cat nose of his sniffing at my workstation, I did my best to answer it.

It was weird, because I always worked alone, except for my coven and Luna. But I didn't mind him being there. His presence, while also the cause of my current distress, seemed to soothe some of the jittery feelings running through me.

I couldn't decide if that was a good thing or a bad thing.

"And what about the object you asked me to bring?" He asked, peering at me curiously.

The ring was sitting in the middle of the desk, untouched.

"I'm going to use it as a talisman. Hopefully, it will protect you and keep this from happening again." I swallowed roughly. If it worked. "You can wear it around your neck, I suppose."

I eyed his cat collar, the one with the bell. "How'd they get that on you, anyway?" Reaching over, I took it off of him, setting it on the table next to me. I should have taken it off sooner. The thought hadn't even occurred to me.

"Around the twelfth time of me chewing it off, I realized it was useless. They just kept putting a new one on me. So I just gave up." He peered down at the orange thing. "Strange, to think I might go back to normal soon." He licked a paw.

"Hopefully," I said, giving what I hoped was an optimistic smile. Even though I had no idea if it would work. If any of it would.

Was I strong enough? Powerful enough?

Maybe I was going overboard, but this was all to get the demon out of my house—out of my life. Wasn't it?

"It will," he said, his voice strong with conviction. "I believe in you."

I turned away, not wanting him to see the warmth on my face.

"What are you doing?"

"Goddess!" I jumped, practically smudging the chalk lines I was drawing on the ground. "Luna! What are you doing here?"

"You didn't respond to my text. It's the full moon—we always spend it together." She pouted.

We did—usually with the coven—but I needed this to work. For Damien's sake. And I couldn't risk them all finding out.

"And also... I brought cupcakes." Luna heaved up the box. My mouth watered at the sight.

"I'm sorry. I just..." I looked down at my partially drawn circle and winced. "Had something I needed to do."

She didn't look surprised. "It's okay, Wil. As long as you're being safe?"

Was I? I was living with a demon in my house, for goodness' sake. Even though he'd been so cute when he'd curled up at my feet last night. When I'd caught him resting his head on my ankle, I'd almost sobbed from how adorable it was.

Sometimes it was hard to remind myself that he wasn't a cat when he snuggled up with me. I'd miss those moments the most.

But maybe he needed it too, that connection—however temporary it was.

As soon as I broke the curse, fixed him, he'd be gone.

"Yeah," I finally said, feeling sadder than I thought I'd feel about that very prospect.

Luna brushed my shoulder. "Do you need anything?"

"I think this is something I have to do alone," I said, straightening my spine. The moment I said the words, the rightness spread through my body.

And I knew I'd spoken the truth. I had to do this alone—for Damien. I couldn't explain why, but it was an undeniable fact.

My sister nodded. "Okay." She looked around the room. "Where's the new cat, anyway? I want to meet him."

I blinked. "He's..." Where was Damien, anyway?

He'd been laying in the patch of sun that came through the

library windows earlier. It made me snort, because only this demon could sunbathe, still claim he *wasn't a cat,* and make it endearing.

The worst part of all of this was I was losing another cat.

Meow. He didn't jingle anymore, since I'd taken that damn collar off.

"Oh! Hello there." Luna bent down, extending her hand out to Damien, who tilted his head as he sniffed her unconvincingly.

"This is my sister," I said to my cat, aware that this was only awkward for me. Because my sister had no idea that the cat who was currently rubbing against her was practically royalty in *Hell.*

"He's friendly."

Damien chirped in response, rubbing against Luna's ankles happily.

Except for when a man *is around,* I thought with a snort, and Damien's head whipped around to look at me.

"Oh, yeah," I finally agreed. "Definitely friendly."

You know, I could still bite you, Damien thought into my mind. *I do have teeth.*

I narrowed my eyes at him, unable to say anything back.

"I'll have to bring Selene over for a playdate," Luna gushed, oblivious to the conversation going on in my mind. Selene was her white, fluffy cat she'd gotten at seven years old.

What seven-year-old was *good* at naming their familiar? I'd named mine *Binx,* after all. And Luna—named after the *moon,* well... she'd named her cat after the Goddess of the moon.

That was my sister for you.

I wondered how my sister's familiar would react to my demon cat. Would she feel that something was wrong with him?

How did cats act around demons, anyway?

Especially ones that could turn into cats?

Still not a cat, Damien interjected.

They well warded Pleasant Grove against evil beings and regular humans, so I'd never met a demon before this. Probably why I was so hesitant to accept Damien's status as one. How did he even get through the barrier?

"Well? What do you think?" Luna asked, drawing me back into the conversation, prying my eyes away from Damien's black form.

I resisted rolling my eyes. If I had any luck, well... he wouldn't *be* a cat after tonight. And definitely not my cat. "Maybe." I agreed, not wanting to commit to anything. Especially if I couldn't figure this out by the next coven meeting, I'd probably have to recruit their help.

We're definitely not doing that.

I leveled a look at him. *Get out of my head,* I wanted to say. But it wasn't like he could read my thoughts.

Sighing, I turned back to my chalk. I'd have to redraw the five-pointed star again later, since Luna's arrival had messed up my focus.

Placing the chalk on the big table in the center of the room, I propped my hip against it, leaning back to watch my sister.

It was crazy how fast she'd become her own person. There was only three years between us, but she'd been my little shadow when we were younger—always wanting to help her big sister, to do whatever I was doing.

But before my eyes, she'd transformed, blossoming into herself. The witch who loved pastels and baking and preferred to surround herself with happy, bright things, instead of our sad, old house.

I knew why she moved out, wanting to live closer to the bakery, but still... I missed her. Though—maybe I was glad she wasn't around right now. Not with what was living under my roof. Or who.

"Are you still lonely all alone in this big house without me?" Luna's mind seemed to track the same way mine did, neither one of us having to say anything.

"It's not so bad now." I could feel my cheeks pink, and I knew Damien's stare was on me without even having to look.

How can she be lonely, Damien thought to me, puffing up his fuzzy chest, *when she has me?*

Four days. It had been four days, and already, I felt like I was used to his presence. I'd known he could talk for half of it, and yet, it already felt weird not being able to respond to him.

"It's not like your bedroom isn't still here. You could always move back." I pinned her with a stare. Her old furniture still sat in the room, extra dresses left in the closet. It still smelled like her, too, somehow, like freshly made pastries and icing.

The same scent that greeted me every morning at the bakery. If I was being honest with myself, it was the reason I was still there. Sure, I owned half—we'd started it with what our parents had left us—but I stayed because it was my connection to my sister.

She tugged at her overall dress as she stood up. "I'm twenty-five, Willow. You don't have to keep taking care of me, I promise. I can take care of myself."

"I just..."

"I know." She sighed. "I know what losing our parents did to you. But I'm okay, really." Luna squeezed my shoulder. "Now, I'll let you carry on with your secret spell." She winked at me. "Don't go chasing after your soulmate without me, Wil."

Barking out a laugh, I shook my head. "That's *not* what I'm doing."

"Sure." She shrugged, giving Damien one last pat on the

head before turning to head out the door. "Whatever you say, sis."

"That's not what I'm doing," I repeated to Damien after she'd left, who'd curled up on the old wooden rocking chair that sat in the room's corner.

He blinked, his cat-like eyes flashing red for only a moment. "I know that." His voice was smooth, deep, and sent a sudden shudder through my spine.

I nodded, saying nothing else.

Maybe I *was* losing my mind.

Damien sat in the middle of the magic circle I'd drawn, each tip of the five-pointed star marked with a white candle. The entire thing was ringed in a thick line of black salt, and the bundles of herbs were burning, wafting over the area.

His little cat nose twitched. "Ready?"

Everything was set. The moon was high in the sky.

All that was left was, well... me.

I nodded, stepping up to the circle. I'd donned a more *traditional* outfit for this, complete with my mother's favorite hat and the black cloak that covered the billowing layers of fabric of my dress.

The words ran through my mind, and I visualized what I was attempting to do before I started. Find the curse, break the chains, set the magic free. Nothing like performing a ceremony on the full moon to add pressure to you.

This had to work.

Why was it so important to me? I didn't know the reason, but I could feel it in my soul, the same way I recognized Luna as my twin flame.

Maybe Damien was an evil being, a demon who didn't belong here in our world, but there was an underlying sadness there that I wanted to understand. That I resonated with myself.

Beginning to chant the spell, I closed my eyes as I visualized my magic pouring out of me. It wasn't often that I used it like this, *undoing* what had been done. Hexes and simple spells wore off. But this curse was different.

It was strong.

I squeezed my palm tight around his mother's ring, grounding me to him, to our connection. I'd already blessed it, placing a protection spell on it and adding a chain so he could wear it around his neck, but it wouldn't be enough. That was obvious now.

In my mind's eye, I could see his spirit, trapped inside the form of the cat, staring up at me. Begging to be freed. The curse was complex. Ropes of magic spun around him, keeping him contained, and I slowly worked to untangle them. To free him from the *thing* that plagued him.

This witch had been powerful, that much I knew.

But, I thought with a smirk, I was more powerful. I could outsmart her.

"Reverse the curse. Break the ties. Let what has come unbidden, be unbound." I said in a voice that wasn't quite my own, and when I opened my eyes, I could *see* the magic flowing freely from my hands, wrapping around Damien's body.

And when the magic ran out, when I finally put my hands down, everything faded into black.

I closed my eyes.

Just a minute, I thought to myself.

Before I passed out.

I was floating on clouds, nestled into a soft, fluffy bed. Warm, comfortable. The feeling of contentment rolled over me. Like everything was peaceful. Happy.

"Willow?" The voice speaking to me sounded so concerned, so... *rough*. At odds with my current senses.

Whimpering, I shook my head. I wanted to stay in this beautiful place. But the voice pulled me in. I peeled my eyes open, blinking back at the dark head of hair looking down at me.

"Damien?" I squeaked out, looking up into a pair of blood-red eyes. "It... worked?"

"Thank fuck."

Of course, he's relieved that it worked.

I sat up, glancing at the bed. Someone had expertly tucked me into the sheets, my favorite fuzzy blanket from the couch wrapped all around me. Oh. I'd—"What happened?" I asked, rubbing my forehead.

The last thing I remembered was unweaving the other witches' curse. Darkness still flooded in through the window, giving me no indication how long I'd been asleep.

He frowned. "You passed out, Willow. I..." A hand rubbed over his face. "You scared me half to death."

I looked at my hands. "I... did?" Maybe I'd channeled more power than I realized last night, because I'd never passed out from using my magic before. It had always come to me with ease. "I didn't know..." I turned my head to the curtains, using a flick of my hand to close them.

Even that movement was straining. My innate magic was

clearly temporarily exhausted. I'd never run so ragged before. Never had a reason to.

Damien made an indistinct sound in his throat, guiding my attention back to him.

"Little witch," he murmured, cupping my jaw with his hand. His voice was rough, like with disuse.

Goddess, help me. I couldn't stop staring at his face. At that jawline, practically sculpted from granite. I'd never imagined my demon cat would look like this. But holy hell, anything I could have imagined paled compared to the actual man sitting in front of me.

My lips tilted up in a small smile.

"I've got you," he promised. "Nothing will happen to you as long as I'm here, Willow. I vow it."

His words sank into my skin.

As long as he was here. But how long would that be?

And why did I not want to see him go?

damien

Fuck. That was the first thought that had sprung to mind as Willow released me from the cursed prison I'd been in.

I'd barely been able to make it to her as her body fell to the ground, practically lifeless. If it hadn't been for my demon abilities—that superhuman speed—I would have lost my shit. Maybe I still was.

Because my heart was racing, even as she gave me a small smile from her bed. I couldn't help myself. That was the only explanation for what slipped out of my mouth.

I've got you. Nothing will happen to you as long as I'm here, Willow. I vow it.

Why had I said those words? Maybe I'd been thinking them, but they slipped out before I could stop myself.

The second I'd gotten my form back, when all of my powers had drawn back into my body, the truth had clicked in place.

Her scent hit me like a lightning bolt to my system. *Mine.*

She was—mine.

How did I not see it sooner? How had that curse clouded my thoughts so fully?

Especially when I *knew* what it was like to find your—

"You're really fine?" Willow's question interrupted my thoughts. Her eyes were wide, the green hue so bright.

"For fuck's sake," I muttered, thrusting my head into my hands. Willow was concerned about *me*? Even though I'd been the one to carry her weak body to this room? "You're the one that was hurt, and you're asking me?"

A small smile curled upon her lips. "You're not a cat."

"I told you I wasn't." My lip twitched. It was hard not to give her the same expression back.

"Still, I couldn't be sure. Who *would* believe a talking cat?"

I chuckled. "Nothing gets past you, little witch, hm?"

Willow yawned, stretching her arms out. "What time is it?"

I glanced at the clock that sat on her bedside table. "Three AM."

"I was out for that long? Gods."

"Yes." My head tipped down in a brief nod.

I'd sat by her bedside for hours, terrified that her breaking my curse had caused some irreparable damage to my witch. What I would do if it had, I didn't know, but... I didn't leave. Even though her scent was intoxicating to my system. I wondered if I was already addicted to it. If the way I craved her, down to my being, was normal.

I needed to keep my distance. To stay away. To not let my primal instincts take over.

I cleared my throat. "Now that I know you're awake, I should let you sleep. We can talk more in the morning."

"Mmm." Willow's eyes drifted closed once more, the ghost of a smile still carved onto her lips.

Stay. The voice crept into my mind, soft and sweet. *Hers.*

Rolling my head back, I let out a sigh of relief. Willow was okay. It would be fine.

And... it was good to be back in my proper form. I flexed my hands, staring at my fingers.

Touching her was bad. I knew it as soon as I had picked her up into my arms, carrying her limp body back to her bedroom, laying her under her comforter and making sure she was comfortable.

Because touching her... was going to make me want more.

And I couldn't give her that. I wasn't worthy of it.

What business did I have coming in here, messing up her life, anyway? She'd adopted a cat, expecting a lifelong feline friend.

Instead, she'd gotten *me*.

A tricky, conniving asshole who wasn't even honest with his purpose here. And yet—I couldn't look away. Couldn't force myself to part from her. Fuck, but I didn't want to.

Maybe I didn't need to come to terms with the truths I'd realized today, but I'd think about those later. About what they meant.

Instead, I'd stay here, just like this—watching her sleep.

"Good morning," Willow said with a yawn, tightening the robe around her waist.

When she saw me standing at her fridge, looking at its contents, she raised an eyebrow. "What are you doing?"

"Making breakfast?" I answered. "What does it look like I'm doing?"

"You... you can cook?"

"Of course I can cook. There's a lot you don't know about me, after all." I smirked.

"Huh." She blinked, as if taking in my form for the first time. Taking in *me*.

I'd never been insecure about my appearance. From a young age, even in the demon realm, they had praised me for my looks. My dark hair and pale skin. But to have Willow's eyes on me, tracing over every inch of my six-foot-six frame, was something completely different.

When I'd shifted back into my form, I'd had half a thought to conjure clothes before scooping her up. I was still wearing that same tight black t-shirt and pants. In all the heyday with making sure she was okay, I hadn't changed this morning. But watching the way her eyes trailed appreciatively down my body, I was almost glad I didn't.

No one had ever looked at me like *that* before. It was a curious stare, like she couldn't believe who stood in her kitchen.

Closing the refrigerator doors so the food wouldn't spoil, I moved to stand in front of her.

"You did it," I confirmed, willing myself not to touch her. To take a step back. I couldn't think straight with her this close to me. Not with her scent invading all of my senses.

How had I not noticed before just how lovely she was? Even with her hair tousled from sleep and in hardly more than pajamas, she was beautiful. I towered over her, and it struck me how much smaller she was than me when I was in this form. *Little* was fitting. In every sense of the word. I had to be at least a foot taller than her.

Maybe it was because it had been so long, but for the first time in my life, I felt like having access to my full powers had completely overwhelmed my senses. Or maybe they were just flooded with *her*. Especially when she was so close to me and looking at me like *that*.

She hummed in response. "I guess I did." Her eyes focused on my face. "How do you feel?"

Even now, Willow was more concerned about me than herself. I didn't know how to feel about that.

"Normal." My powers thrummed through my body again, my access no longer limited. I let a sliver of darkness weave through my fingers before turning my attention back to her. "What about you?"

Her cheeks turned an adorable shade of pink. "I'm okay. Really. I didn't know using that much magic would overwhelm me. But I feel fine this morning. Thank you." She bobbed her head. Shook it. "You didn't have to stay, you know?"

"What do you mean?" I murmured, my hand moving to cup her jaw. *How could I not?*

"Damien..." Her voice was quiet, but—*sweet*.

I removed my hand from her face. Fuck. I couldn't keep touching her like this.

Distance. I needed distance from her. Clearing my throat, I changed the subject. "What do you want to do today, little witch?"

She looked surprised. "Today...?"

I quirked an eyebrow. "Well, after feeding you, I was thinking maybe you could show me around town."

"But... I thought... Don't you have to leave?" She trailed off. There was a hint of sadness in her eyes that I didn't think that I'd imagined. Like maybe she didn't want me to leave, either.

So I'd stay. Of course I'd stay. How could I leave her?

"Not right away."

My body thrummed with the decision. With the *rightness*.

Maybe I was supposed to be here. There was obviously a reason I'd ended up here, in this town. I'd been tracking signatures of magic, looking for *her*. So maybe it was okay that I stayed.

She perked up. "Really?"

"I was thinking about staying for a month or so." Clearing my throat, I finally moved away from her. "There's still some... unfinished business I have here, actually."

Something that started with a *W*.

Now that I was back in my form, I needed to focus on my mission. Not on the witch in front of me. But fuck if she wasn't alluring. I didn't want to part from her.

Willow raised an eyebrow. "Really? Here in Pleasant Grove?"

I nodded. "Yes. So, I'll just stay with you. Lay low while I fi—."

"What? No." Willow interrupted, suddenly flabbergasted. "You can't stay *here*."

But she hadn't wanted me to go before, had she? Yet, she looked flustered; her face an even brighter shade of pink than before.

"It was fine before."

"Yeah, well, before, you were a *cat*."

Smirking, I leaned in closer towards her. "I can go back to being a cat if you want." *I* didn't want that, but I knew there wasn't a chance I was leaving her. Not like this. Not after last night. "And I still owe you a favor." For helping me. Freeing me from being stuck in that form.

"That's not how this works. We didn't make a deal. You don't owe me anything."

"Willow." I sighed. She was so stubborn, and damn it, I *liked* that. It was joining my ever-growing list of things I liked about my little witch. "I just..." I looked around her house. What was it about this place that made me feel so at *home?*

"Just for a few weeks, and then I'll be out of your hair. We can be... roommates."

"Roommates?" She raised an eyebrow. "What's the magic word?"

I grit my teeth. *You've got to be kidding me.* What was I, a five-year-old? "*Please.*"

Her light brown locks framed her face, somehow making that little scowl she was wearing look endearing. I liked it. More than I wanted to admit.

"Okay. You can sleep on the couch," she finally agreed, crossing her arms over her chest, doing her best to look menacing. It failed, because no matter what she did, the little witch managed to look adorable.

The couch. I snorted. "Fine."

Willow's lips widened, her teeth peeking out as she gave me a dazzling grin. "That was easier than I thought."

"What?"

"To have you begging me."

You'd like that, would you? Me on my knees for you.

"All you have to do is ask, witch."

"Mm. You'd like that, would you, demon?"

My hand curled around her bicep. "Be careful what you ask for."

Something passed between us. Her eyes flickered from my hand on her arm, up to my face, and down to my lips. I didn't think I missed the heat there, but as much as I wanted to... *No.*

It was too soon for that.

Prying my fingers from her skin, I turned back to her kitchen. "So... What do you want for breakfast? I've fried up a mean egg or two. As long as it's not seafood. I don't have much of a stomach for that. Not after so long as a cat."

When I looked at her again, she was still standing frozen in the same place, her eyes wide. "You're really staying?" Her words were quiet, barely more than a whisper.

"Do you want me to?"

Maybe that was the more important question.

Her eyes met mine, and she gave me a small, single nod. The movement was almost too slight to catch, but I couldn't miss it. Not when I was so focused on her.

"Okay. It's settled then." I crossed my arms over her shoulders. "I'm staying in Pleasant Grove." *With you,* I didn't say.

Clearly unfazed by my statement, Willow just gave me another dip of her head to acknowledge my response before turning around. "I'm going to shower."

"What about breakfast?" I shouted after her, willing my feet to stay put. Not to follow her into her bathroom. Not to think about Willow in the shower. *Fuck me.*

"We'll eat in town!" She hollered back. "I have to go to the bakery, anyway!"

A moment later, I heard the shower water turn on, and I sank into the chair.

What the hell was I doing?

I had a mission to think about. Except any time I was near her, every thought of that slipped my mind, and it was just *her.*

Long, brown hair tumbling down her back. Bright green eyes staring into mine. There was a lightness in them I'd never felt before. I wanted to experience it, too.

Groaning, I looked down at my rumpled clothes. If we were going into town, I'd probably need more than this. Human temperatures didn't affect me much, but people often looked at you strangely if you didn't match the locals. Although in a town of witches, I wondered if anything would be odd to wear around them.

Was I really doing this? Sauntering into town on the arm of

a witch, knowing I absolutely shouldn't? Her kind hated me. And yet... I couldn't imagine letting her out of my sight.

So if she was going to work, I'd follow her. Make sure she was safe. Protect her from anyone who looked her way.

It wasn't the first time she was taking me into town, and yet this time, it was different.

Maybe because I wasn't a cat—I was back on my own two legs, with my wits about me. Or maybe it was the way something had happened, changed between us.

Did she feel it too?

I exited that line of thought as quickly as I'd entered it. I couldn't afford to be distracted from my mission. Not when so much was at stake.

Leave no rock unturned, brother, he'd instructed me.

I'd trekked through dozens of witch towns, but the identity of *her* remained elusive to me.

I snorted with the thought of how mad he'd be when he found out I'd wasted a month stuck in feline form. My brother didn't share the trait, though he had other powers. His mother wasn't a shifter like mine had been.

So deep in thought, it was her scent that startled me out of my stupor instead of the sight of her, her long brown hair down in a loose braid.

"You ready? I'm starving." She asked, still tugging on the bottom of her boot. When her eyes landed on me, she froze. "You changed."

I cleared my throat. "Yes."

"Huh." She peered up at me, a curious expression having settled over her face.

"What, Willow?"

"Do you... know how to glamor yourself?"

There was something about Damien like this that I had a hard time keeping my eyes off of. Where he'd gotten his clothes from, I had no idea. Somehow he looked perfectly natural here in his pair of denim jeans, tight black shirt, and black leather jacket. It was effortlessly *hot*.

When was the last time I'd been this attracted to another person? Years.

Tugging on the bottom of my forest-green sweater dress— one of my favorites, because it made my eyes pop—I attempted to pull it further down my thighs. I'd pulled on a pair of fleece-lined tights with it and my favorite heeled booties, but suddenly I felt completely out of sorts.

Maybe it was his demon magic. There had to be a reason they warned witches to stay away from them, right? That was what was making me feel like this.

Like I was seconds from coming out of my skin.

"What's on your mind, little witch?" Damien asked, catching me staring.

"Oh." My cheeks practically flushed pink. "Nothing."

Except I could smell his cologne from where I stood by his

side, wafting into my nostrils like the most intoxicating smell on the planet. I couldn't even pin down the scent: some mixture of pine, musk, and smoke, but it seemed to envelop my entire being.

There was a part of me that wanted to pretend that everything was as usual—I came this way every day to go to the bakery, after all.

Except today was anything but ordinary. And Damien was a constant reminder of that.

His soothing voice shook me from my inane thoughts. "So, you normally walk into town?"

"Huh?" I wasn't expecting the question. Or, rather, I wasn't expecting small talk at all. Once I'd processed his question, I nodded. "When the weather's nice. It's not very far, and I always love walking this path."

It was one perk of living in such a small community— being able to walk almost everywhere. I *had* a car, but I didn't use it unless I had to drive all the way to the other end of town. Mainly, I drove when I needed to go into the closest human city for something, like getting our coffee machines repaired.

Today, the air was crisp and clear, just a hint of rain that clung around, and it relaxed me. That and the crunch of the leaves littered on the ground made for the perfect fall day.

"I see." Damien shoved his hands in his pockets, and I turned away, not wanting to look like I was still staring at his face. Even if I was obsessed with it.

I hummed in response, thinking about what I was going to say to Luna when I stopped at the bakery. *'I'm sorry'* didn't quite cut it, but I owed my sister an apology after I'd ditched her so much these past few days.

Besides, I still owed her that trip to the bar.

"So you like it here, living in this town?" He looked around, surveying the houses that sat right at the edge of downtown.

Main Street, full of small businesses and cornerstone witchy establishments, was only a block away.

Nodding, I tried to look at the town through the eyes of a stranger. Wondering what this place might look like to someone new. "I've lived here all my life. My coven and I grew up together. Most of us only left for college, and even then, we moved back. It's hard being a witch and not living in the community."

There was too much at stake. And no one would under-stand—except I thought Damien might. Not being able to practice magic, for fear of someone seeing you—that was the true curse of the outside world. Maybe a higher education wasn't *necessary*—several of the witches I'd grown up with had simply learned their family's trade and never left town.

But I'd appreciated the world-view I'd gained by going into the human world for those years. It was before my parents had died, so I hadn't felt as bad about leaving Luna. But now... I couldn't imagine not being by her side.

"All my best friends are in the coven," I continued. "There's thirteen of us, and they're practically family."

It was a perfect number: thirteen. My mom and her friends had all belonged to a smaller coven, and all ended up having kids during the same few years. There had never been another idea when it came time to form ours.

The humans had Girl Scout Troops, and we had our coven. We learned magic together, practiced together, discovered what our innate gifts were together. I'd never once taken them for granted. And I'd always had my sister—even with the three years between us, she was still my best friend—by my side.

"What about your parents? Where are they at?"

I cast my gaze to my feet, my voice growing smaller. "They're gone." Sometimes, I wished I could imagine that they were just off on vacation. Seeing the world. Enjoying them-selves. That was easier than the reality.

"Oh. I'm sorry to hear that."

Shaking my head, I willed myself not to look at him. If I did, I'd probably cry. And I didn't want to mourn my parents. Not today. I just wanted to enjoy myself for once.

Pasting a somber smile on my face, I watched as my town came into full view. And I let the jack-o'-lanterns, paper ghosts, and string lights distract me from the rest of the thoughts rattling around in my mind.

Like the subject of my once-cat-turned-demon, followed by the man himself. The stranger, I tried to remind myself—who was currently walking beside me.

I kept my eyes pinned to the ground, trying to force myself not to keep from staring at his face. At the eyes I knew he'd changed to a deep-chocolate brown, which somehow seemed endless. Like if I stared into them long enough, I could find answers to questions I hadn't even thought to ask yet.

At least he didn't look like a demon, even if he still stood taller than any human man I'd ever seen, and the physique his body sported was *unreal*. He was a foot taller than me, and even with my heeled boots, I still felt impossibly short.

Something I was trying very hard not to focus on. There was no reason for me to think about it—how good he looked, simply strolling down the street beside me.

But even as I crunched over leaves in my heeled booties—I knew there was no way to ignore the way I could *feel* him next to me.

How was it possible that I could find his very nearness so comforting after only a few days? He was a stranger to me, in every way, and yet it felt like there was nowhere else I would rather be.

I cleared my throat. "After I help out at the bakery for a bit,

I was thinking I could show you around town. And then tonight, if you wanted to go... there's the Pumpkin Festival." I looked up at him under my lashes.

"The Pumpkin Festival?" Damien raised an eyebrow, shaking his head in amusement.

"Mhm. We normally have a booth, serving pumpkin hot chocolate, pumpkin coffee, and Luna's famous cookies."

"Let me guess, they're pumpkin too?"

I couldn't help the giggle that slipped out. "Yes. But also, she makes regular sugar cookies too—those are just pumpkin shaped." I was almost drooling, just thinking about her cookies. Not a single person in town could bake like my sister. "There's also a pumpkin patch, hayrides, a pie-eating contest, and at the end of the night there's a..."

Looking over, I expected to find Damien watching our surroundings, but I found him hanging on my every word. "There's a what?"

He brushed a piece of hair back behind my ear, and I suddenly wished I'd worn my hat, if only so I could hide my face behind the brim. I wasn't used to this much scrutiny or attention from... anyone. Let alone from a handsome man.

"A dance. Old Mrs. Whittle lets the town use her barn, and The Enchanted Cauldron sets up a bar, and... What?"

Damien's lips curled up into a smile. "Has anyone ever told you how your face lights up when you're excited about something?"

"Oh." Was my whole face on fire? It had to be.

Oh my god. I felt like I had bats fluttering around in my stomach. When was the last time a gorgeous stranger flirted with me?

Never. The answer was never.

"Anyway, I, uh... Do you want to go?"

He frowned. "To the dance?"

"Mhm. And the festival."

"I don't really..." Was it me, or did he look almost... embarrassed? "Do stuff like that."

"Dance?" I asked.

Damien shook his head. "I, uh..." Oh, he was *definitely* embarrassed. It made me feel strangely at ease. Maybe because he felt as out of his element as I did with him. "I'm not very good at socializing. I've never been around that many humans before."

"I can teach you." I peeked over my shoulder at him, wanting to gauge his reaction. "If you want." It surprised me how easily the offer slipped out of my mouth, but even more so how easily he agreed.

"Okay. Show me around your town, and then to this pumpkin festival. You just have to promise me something."

"Anything." There was no part of me that didn't beam at his agreement. About getting to show someone else this place that I loved so much.

He leaned in close, his mouth inches away from my ear. "Don't leave me alone."

"I won't." I gave him a shy nod as the bakery came into view.

It suddenly occurred to me that I still had no idea what to tell my sister. Or anyone else.

What would people think when they saw the two of us together? It was a small town, and people talked. Gossip would spread, especially when I hadn't been with anyone since college. And even then—I'd never brought a boyfriend home. Even when my parents were alive.

I cleared my throat. "So, what's the story here?"

"What story?" Damien raised an eyebrow at me as I gestured between us.

65

"How we met. Why I'm wandering around town with a handsome stranger that no one's ever seen before."

His voice popped into my mind. *You think I'm handsome?*

"Stop doing that."

Damien shrugged. "I wasn't aware we needed a cover story. We can't just be two people strolling down Main Street, looking at the decor?"

"My sister will ask questions." *Everyone* would ask questions. Questions I didn't have answers to yet.

"Mmm."

"Damien." I rubbed my temples. "This is serious."

"You worry too much, little witch."

Yeah, well, maybe you don't worry enough.

Nonsense. I just worry about the important things.

I stopped in the middle of the sidewalk, and Damien turned around to face me, raising an eyebrow. "What?"

I crossed my arms over my chest. "I... thought you said you couldn't read my mind."

"I can't." He looked confused for a moment. "What do you mean?"

"You're joking, right?" *I didn't say that out loud.* "And you answered me."

He searched my face, and I wondered if he found whatever answer he was looking for there.

How come we can communicate with our minds? Silence was my only answer.

"Why did I think you were actually going to answer me?" I grumbled to myself. There were some witches who had... abilities, but nothing like this. It certainly wasn't anything *I'd* experienced before. Even with Luna, sometimes it felt like I could anticipate what she was going to say before she said it. But she was my sister—my *Twin Flame.* Of course, I was in tune with her feelings.

66

None of that explained this.

I started moving again, my demon-cat-turned-human matching my pace, stride for stride.

"No one's ever come with me to the festival before," I admitted, my voice low. "I don't know what they'll think."

"Your friends?"

I nodded. "And my coven."

"Right." He winced, as if it was a sudden reminder of our standings in this town. That I was a witch, and he was a *demon*. "And why can't we tell them the truth?"

My jaw fell open in shock. "No one's going to believe that." Watching to make sure I didn't step on any cracks on the pavement—definitely not because I was avoiding watching his face —I continued on. "Besides. One witch already cursed you. My kind... they don't trust demons. I'm not sure I'll be able to fix it if it happens again. Do you really want to advertise who you are?"

"You're not going to tell your sister?"

"No."

"But aren't you... close? She even came over to check on you yesterday." He frowned.

She normally came over a few times throughout the week. It was her old house too, after all. And we worked together.

What would I say when she inevitably asked me why *Damien* the cat was gone and *Damien* the not-human was strolling around our town with me?

"We can be close and still keep secrets from each other. Important secrets. Don't you have them with your siblings?"

His voice was quiet, withdrawn. "I've never really had anything to hide. My brother..." Damien shook his head. "It's not like that. My life's never really been *my own*." When I looked over at him, he'd focused his eyes on a distant spot in the background.

"Oh." That sounded... sad. And lonely. Suddenly, a lot of things made sense to me about him. Why he didn't seem to want to leave my side, and why he was in no rush to go back to the demon realm. He said he had unfinished business here, didn't he? Was it presumptuous of me to hope that it was just *me?*

Was I the first friend he'd ever had? It seemed strange to call him that, since I'd known him less than a week, but it felt right. Better than strangers.

A thought occurred to me, and I let it slip out before thinking better of it. "How old are you?"

"Two hundred and eighty-seven."

"What?" I hadn't expected that.

"Aging works differently in the demon realm." He shrugged. "In human terms, I'm not even close to middle-aged yet."

"Wow. I can't even imagine living that long."

What kind of existence had he been living for the past almost three centuries? I hardly knew anything about him as a being, but I got the idea his years weren't full of happiness, love, laughter—*life.* And for whatever reason, I wanted to show him what that was like. What it was like to grow up here in Pleasant Grove.

I let the quiet blanket over us, save for the leaves crunching under our feet and the wind blowing through the trees. At least I could appreciate the decorations this way. It was the reason I still enjoyed walking into town, even when the air was nippy. Most of the residents had decorated their houses, lights and fake cobwebs and carved pumpkins that sat on their stoops. I still needed to get my own—Luna and I normally went to the pumpkin patch the first day it opened, but we hadn't yet this year.

Luna. I let loose a long sigh.

"Never mind," I mumbled. "How we met doesn't matter, anyway."

"Why not?"

"Because my sister... She's a seer. And is *incredibly* perceptive. I can't get anything past her."

There really was no point in trying to hide who he was to her. Maybe for the rest of the town's sake, I could pretend he was just a friend, but my sister wouldn't buy that. My coven would know that I hadn't met him at a bar—though I wasn't sure I wanted the implication of *that,* anyway.

Even if he was handsome. I peeked at him again, catching a wistful look on his face.

I was trying to imagine what my life would have looked like if he'd always been here. A part of this town. If we'd spent the last few Halloweens carving pumpkins together and sipping hot apple cider as we walked through the corn maze.

My heart ached, and that was what startled me out of those thoughts. I had no business thinking about Damien like that.

Like he was *mine.*

He wasn't even my cat anymore, after all.

That left a sour taste in my mouth. I ran my arms over my shoulders.

"Willow." His voice was low, soothing, as his hand wrapped around my wrist. "Where'd you go?"

"What?" I looked up into his eyes, full of concern. For me? Or for himself?

The warmth of his grip flowed through me, grounding me in the moment. I hated that I liked it so much. I wasn't supposed to like *him.* He was a demon, after all.

Every witch's mortal enemy. What did I think was going to happen, bringing him into town?

"This is a mistake." I pulled away, loosening his grip from

my arm. "You should go. That way you don't put yourself in danger again just to..."

I froze, looking up at him. All six and a half feet of him. He was looking at me with an emotion I couldn't read in his eyes. And for the first time, I so badly wanted to hear his thoughts. To know what he was thinking.

Maybe it didn't work that way, but I couldn't help wanting more of him.

"No." He moved startlingly fast, and then his hands were on my face. Cupping my cheeks. Holding me, so reverently. I wasn't sure I'd ever been touched like that before. "I'm not leaving. Not yet."

"Okay." The breath I released was quiet, almost inconsequential. Except...

My lips parted as I stared up at Damien. There was no way I could stop my gaze from dropping to his lips. Full and *pouty* and begging for attention. They looked soft, and I wondered what they'd feel like on mine.

Why was I lusting after this man who was practically a stranger to me? I moved to step back, and his hands slipped from my face, severing whatever connection we'd shared.

"Come on. Luna's expecting me." I'd been a shitty co-owner this week. I needed to make it up to her somehow.

And I needed to distance myself from the demon at my side before I got attached. Or worse.

Because he'd be leaving eventually.

The bell jingled as I pulled open the door to the shop, the scent of cookies baking instantly hitting my nose.

"Willow!" My little sister's face lit up in a bright smile

when she saw me, making me feel even guiltier for the past few days.

"Hi, Luna."

She had a little dusting of flour on her cheek, and more covering the pink pastel apron she was wearing covered in little cartoon ghosts. Her honey blonde hair, a trait inherited from our mom, was pulled up into a messy bun with one of her signature printed bandanas, but her smile quickly faded when she noticed the dark shadow that was still glued to my side.

Damien was frozen, his face drained of all color as he stared at my sister.

I frowned. What was wrong with both of them? "Damien, this is my sister, Luna." I elbowed him in the stomach, hoping he would resemble more of a human, settling my face into a small smile as I turned back to Luna. "Luna, this is Damien. My... friend."

Stepping closer to us, she held out her hand over the counter, schooling her expression into a smile. "It's very nice to meet you, Damien."

He stiffened, only staring at her hand and making no move to offer his own. After a moment of silence, he looked away.

"I have to go," he muttered, turning around.

Walking out without another word to me. Luna's hand was still in the air.

"But..." I frowned, the bell chiming once more.

Leaving the two of us standing in silence.

"What was that about?" Luna asked, turning her head.

"I don't..." I shook my head. "I don't know. He's..."

We were supposed to spend the day together. And now he was just... gone?

Maybe *he* didn't want to be here with me, after all. Maybe I was just a means to an end, and whatever. All those questions earlier...

I shook my head, dislodging the thoughts. At least I had my sister by my side.

"Come on," Luna said, pulling me into the back. She filled a bowl with ingredients for frosting as I hopped up on a counter. I needed to start working, and I hadn't even eaten breakfast yet, but I was too confused to focus on any of that.

Instead, I watched her work.

"So, did it work?"

"Hm?"

"Your spell." She raised an eyebrow. "From last night?"

"Oh." I was glad I couldn't see out the window, because I knew I'd just be looking for him. "Yeah."

"Can't help but notice your new... *friend* has the same name as your new cat." She smirked, starting up the stand mixer to beat the bowl of frosting.

I busied myself by tying my apron and ignoring her question.

I didn't have an answer for her anyway.

Because how on earth was I going to explain to her that I was spending time with a *demon*?

*W*hat the fuck.

I shut my eyes, trying to process everything. The woman I'd come here to find—it couldn't be Willow's *sister*. Not after everything we'd already gone through. And yet... I'd taken one look at her and felt the power radiating off of her, and I *knew*.

Dammit. I needed more time.

To get to know Willow, to get to experience all the things I'd never imagined I would ever get to do. It was so simple, and yet...

My hands raked through my hair as I paced in the back alley, trying to make sense of everything.

Why had I headed here in the first place? I'd felt like something had pulled me here, and once she'd found me, I thought maybe that something was Willow.

But... *Luna*? Her sister?

I hadn't been able to detect it in cat form—thanks to my senses being cloudy, but it was clear as day now.

Growing up in the demon realm, I'd always heard about

what it was like when you found *the one*. But I'd never imagined I'd actually experience it for myself, to find my—

"Shit."

Pain tugged at the tether between me and Zain, and I knew I could only ignore his call for so long. But to go back to the demon realm, to reveal everything I knew to him... how could I ever do that?

Willow would never forgive me.

And any chance I had with her... It would be over before it started.

She needed some time with her sister. And I needed space to think.

And... A trip to the demon realm.

To see my brother.

I groaned. Today was not going at all like I'd wanted it to.

For starters, I hadn't even made sure Willow had gotten food. And then I'd ran out of there without even explaining to her *why*.

Brushing aside those strange instincts, I made my way down the alley, trying to ignore the tug in my blood as long as I could.

Gritting my teeth, I cursed out. "You just don't know when to stop, do you?"

Looking around to make sure no one was watching me, I stepped into the shadows—transporting myself back home for the first time in months.

"Brother. You've returned." Zain, the crown prince of the demon realm, was perched atop his throne. My brother. He looked so much like me—down to his dark hair and tall stature —but we couldn't have been more different. Especially in our temperaments.

We'd grown up as half-brothers, but sometimes I still felt like a stranger looking at him. He wore a coat of black, adorned with gold and all the finest trimmings befitting a prince, whereas I stood in my human clothes—a t-shirt, leather jacket, and jeans.

Standing in front of him, I crossed my arms over my chest. "You summoned me?"

Our blood tied us together in ways I couldn't even begin to explain.

"Where have you been? We were worried."

Sure, they were.

"You could say I've been a little... tied up." In a cage. By humans.

But I wouldn't expand on where I'd been, or how *exactly* I'd ended up stuck in my other form. If he wanted those memories, he could pry them from my head himself.

His eyes flashed with amusement. "Ah, yes. I trust you had an... enjoyable time?"

If only you knew the half of it. I raised an eyebrow. "Sure. You could say that."

"It's good to see you, you know," Zain said. "It's not the same here without you."

"You're the one who sent me out into the human world to do your bidding. If you wanted to see me, there were easier ways."

Chuckling, my brother settled back into his chair—three steps up on the dais, perched in front of me. Reminding me exactly where I factored in this equation of ours.

Below him.

Never mind how powerful I was, how much control I had over the darkness—power I'd inherited from my father. The shadows were like a second nature to me, the way I could manipulate and create from nothing.

I was the bastard child, and not the chosen one to rule.

Not that I wanted it, anyway. This place hadn't felt like home in a long time.

If I was being honest, I preferred the animal shelter I'd been living at for the past month to my brother's palace in the demon realm.

And I liked Willow's home a thousand times more than both of them.

"And? Was your mission successful? Or have you been *enjoying* yourself a little too much?"

"I need more time," I grit out, not answering him. I needed that time with Willow.

Zain's eyes narrowed. "Damien. Did you find her?"

I couldn't lie to him—but I didn't want this to be the end of my time in Pleasant Grove, either. Instead, I simply nodded.

The worst part was that I *had* found her. And he knew it.

Damn demon magic. I hated that I'd ever had to connect myself to him in that way.

"So, what's the problem?"

There was no easy way around it. "I can't do it." Deliver her to this place like some sort of prized trophy—it felt more like bringing a lamb to the slaughter. An innocent, adorable little lamb.

"It's your sworn duty." To him.

I scoffed. "I liked you better when you weren't an insufferable crown prince."

"Ah, brother. That's where you're wrong—because I've *always* been the insufferable crown prince."

"Nice to see you, too." I rolled my eyes

He stood up, walking down the steps, and slapping a hand against my shoulder. All pretenses gone, *there* was the brother I had grown up with. When we were both still young, and things hadn't been so... tense.

But that was what a few hundred years did to you. You

grew apart. Or you were forced to serve your younger brother for eternity.

You know—*semantics*.

"One month."

I blinked. "What?" It was eerie how that was the same time frame I'd given Willow this morning. Narrowing my eyes, I stared at my brother.

"Whatever you're doing that's distracting you... You can have one more month. And then I expect you to bring her here, to me, and return to my side."

"But—"

Zain tilted his head to the side. "Does some part of that not work for you, brother?"

I ground my teeth together in an effort to not speak back to him. "Fine."

His sharp canine teeth peeked out of his smile this time as he settled back into the chair.

"Don't get distracted this time, Damien. I'll be waiting." There was a strange look in his eye as I turned away, giving him only the wave of my hand as a goodbye, before I created another portal—back to the human world.

Back to my little witch.

I let the shadows cloak around me, hiding me from view as I watched her flit around the shop Willow and her sister owned. This time, I could fully take in the front of their shop. The sign above the door read *The Witches' Brew* and featured an intricately carved cauldron of bubbling coffee.

One of them had taped little bats to the inside of the windows, with the entire storefront fully decked out in

Halloween decor. Fake cobwebs, little orange lights that lined the door frame, and even the sandwich board out front read *'stop by for a brew!'*

It was clear they didn't need the advertising. Downtown Pleasant Grove was small and bustling, and it felt like half of the town must have popped inside since we'd first arrived this morning.

Letting my darkness dissipate, I opened the door, shoving my hands in my pockets as I stood, watching them talk behind the counter.

"Olivia, I have your pumpkin scone and Witch's Cold Brew!" Willow called out as she handed a small paper bag and a cup of coffee to a customer at the counter with a smile. Tucking a brown lock of hair behind her ear, she turned to the next person in line.

She hadn't noticed me yet, and I liked that I could study her like this. Unabashedly, without worrying about what anyone else thought.

There was a pull to her I couldn't explain, a kind of magnetism that drew me in.

I rubbed a hand over my face. This was crazy. There was no way.

Even from here, her sweet scent wafted into my nostrils, and it was all I could do to resist burying my face in her hair and inhaling it.

I wanted her. With every fiber of my being.

But I didn't deserve her. How could I ever deserve someone as perfect, as untouched by hatred and destruction?

She was *mine,* and I knew that down to the depths of my soul—whatever part of it still existed—but she didn't need me.

Fuck.

Willow's gaze connected with mine, and I could feel my

face softening as she walked over to me, the irritation clear on her face.

I had to fix this. I had to make her understand I hadn't *wanted* to go. Even if I couldn't tell her the truth yet. No matter how badly I wanted to.

"I'm sorry."

Throwing myself into the bakery was my best course of action after Damien's sudden disappearance. Once the morning rush was over, I took the time to sweep the entire storefront, leaving no corner untouched. Not only had I finished all the dishes, but I had also wiped down all the tables.

I'd given up on pretending that I wasn't staring out the window for him to come back.

The worst part was I felt like a lovesick fool, consumed by emotions I couldn't control. His vow to stay echoed in my mind, but a small voice inside me wondered if it was true.

Sighing, I turned back to the counter, brewing a fresh pot of coffee while I made an apple cider latte for one of our regulars.

"Is everything ready for tonight?" I asked Luna, who was sliding another tray of freshly baked cookies into the rack to cool. I checked the time. It was almost noon, which meant more than half of our day was already over.

She wiped her hands on her apron. "That's the last of the cookies I had to make. Everything else should be ready to go. You're still going to make the hot chocolate, right?"

The bell on the door chimed, as I called out another customer's order, handing them their drink and pastry.

I nodded. "Of course. And I'm sorry for bailing so much this last week." I'd already prepped everything I'd need for tonight, so when everything was set up, it would just need to be stirred and heated up.

Luna rested her head against my shoulder. "It's okay. I know you've had your hands full with that one."

That one? I looked over at her, and she raised her eyebrows, tilting her head towards the door.

Damien was standing there, looking sheepish and a little guilty.

Walking over to him, I crossed my arms over my chest, ready to tell him off for ditching me, but his expression was full of so much pain that it stopped me in my tracks.

"I'm sorry."

I blinked, not expecting that. "For what?"

"Disappearing." He shook his head. "I had to go... back."

Even though I'd told him so much about my life, and my love for this town, I didn't know the first thing about his home. The demon realm. If he'd had to go back, that must have meant something was seriously wrong.

"Is everything okay?"

Damien's eyes drifted over to Luna in the background, before he turned his attention back to me. "It will be. I'll explain everything later, I promise." He wove our fingers together. "But first, I owe you a date."

"A date?" My cheeks pinked. "I mean, breakfast, yes, but..."

He nodded, kissing my knuckles. "Yes. A date."

Oh. "Oh." I turned back to look at Luna, but she just shook her head with a smile, turning back to her tray of cookies. A silent permission. "Okay. Let me just..."

I looked down at my apron, thanking the Goddess that I

hadn't covered it in coffee or flour. Quickly pulling it off over my head, I returned it to my hook, stopping to let Eryne know I'd be heading out before waving goodbye to Luna.

"Shall we?" Damien offered me his hand once again. I ignored the rush of warmth to my face at taking it.

"Where to?"

"How about we finally get to that tour now?"

I nodded, happily pulling him out of the store—our hands still intertwined.

And for whatever reason, even knowing it would probably lead to disappointment, I didn't want to let go.

We spent the rest of the afternoon wandering through all of downtown. I showed Damien some of my favorite shops, including my favorite bookshop—*Broomsticks and Books*. It had mostly stopped carrying the former, leaving the shop full of magical tombs and regular books alike. Luna loved the romance section, while I loved looking for new recipes tucked amongst the cookbooks here.

Hardly anyone needed broomsticks for transportation anymore. Most of us witches had one sitting in our house, regardless. You never knew when you might need a magical flying broom, after all.

Damien had given me a snort when I told him that.

Next was the ever-changing *Magical Curiosities*: a shop that sold just that, though I'd found quite my share of trinkets there over the years. It was like a thrift store for magical artifacts and witchy goods. My trusty hat had come from there, as well as my black boots with little buttons up the side.

As we walked down Main, we passed by a few more shops: *Dark Moon Fashions,* where I got all my favorite dresses; *Pleasant Grove Realty,* where any witch could find a perfect home; and *Hexed Home Renos*—newly opened and run by two twin witches, Tammy and Talley. They'd been toying with the idea for years, and finally opened it after the rest of our coven told them they'd stop speaking to them if they didn't.

Tough love worked.

My demon companion scratched his head, standing in front of the last one on the street. "What's with the name?"

It'd been Grey's Supermarket for as long as I'd been alive—run by the Grey's, now an older couple whose kids had grown and moved away.

"It's so... normal."

"What?" I laughed. "It's just a supermarket. Do you think we come up with puns for every business here?"

Sure—most of the businesses downtown had cute, kitschy names, but they also catered to the witches that came to visit. We were only an hour outside of Salem, after all. Even if horrible things had happened there, the legacy was strong. Still, there were plenty of normally named establishments in town.

Damien shrugged. "Witches are weird." And wasn't that the understatement of the century?

"This is my favorite spot down here," I murmured, staring at the town gazebo, complete with its own decorations.

His eyes swept across the view before settling back on me. "It's nice."

"When I was younger, I used to come out here and just people watch. It was nice, even when things got busy, to come here and just... slow down. Appreciate life."

Tilting my head, I watched him. I wondered what sort of life he'd led. If he'd ever experienced any moments like that. Blissful peace—quiet happiness. It was a strange thing to ponder, but the tortured look in his eye made me think maybe he hadn't.

Maybe that was one reason he talked little about himself or his life.

"Are you hungry?" I finally asked, breaking the silence.

That was how we ended up sitting at the bar of *The Enchanted Cauldron* for lunch. We'd both ordered burgers, and if I was being honest... it surprised me at how normal it felt with him by my side. Even in college, I'd never felt this comfortable with another person besides Luna or the other members of my coven.

Maybe it was because of the way he'd watched over me all night when I'd passed out. He could have just left. Instead, he didn't leave my side.

I happily chowed down on my burger, noting the look of satisfaction on Damien's face as I ate.

He finished his before mine, though that was partially due to how many people came over to say hi to me. I'd always been a chatty person, and knowing almost everyone in this town didn't help with that.

They were all curious about the man seated by my side, even if they hadn't said it straight out.

"Do you want me to scare them all away so you can eat?" He grunted, taking a sip of his drink.

"No, it's okay. They'll stop eventually. They're just curious about you."

My cheeks warmed at the thought that he cared enough to do that. That he seemed to want to take care of me.

I *was* starving, though, even though I'd definitely eaten a muffin and a few scones while I'd been at the bakery. Even I had to admit that Damien's glares at the other patrons helped to stave them off.

"Thanks," I finally said after I'd finished the last bite of my burger, sucking the extra ketchup that had spilled onto my fingers. "That hit the spot."

Damien looked at his empty tray. I still had a bunch of fries left, but he'd already eaten it all.

"That was... surprisingly good."

I scrunched up my nose. "Were you doubting it would be?"

He chuckled. "No. It's just... the other communities I've been in weren't like this. And they didn't have food nearly this good."

"That's Pleasant Grove for you," I beamed. "It might not be much, but... It's home."

I looked around the bar. The Enchanted Cauldron had been around for generations. Despite the foot traffic this place saw —on account of it being one of the few restaurants in our little community, let alone our only bar—it was still in good shape.

They'd hung all sorts of witchy paraphernalia in here over the years, some as gags, and some that dated back to the Salem Witch Trials themselves. The low lighting from the various lanterns created a cozy atmosphere, and the old-timey portraits on the back walls added a touch of history to the room. There were candles on the shelves that looked like they'd burned and had melted into place—like no one had ever bothered to clean up the wax. But my favorite part was the Morgans, who'd bought the bar last year and spruced it up, had even added little cauldrons filled with succulents to each table.

"I can see why you love it." His words brought a smile to my face, and I couldn't stop myself from beaming. "Thank you for showing it to me today." Damien said it like he knew what it meant to me.

"It was my pleasure," I said, blushing. "So, what do you think? Still want to stick around?" I nudged him with my shoulder, scooting my barstool closer to his.

Part of me was hoping he'd say yes. That he didn't want to leave, either. That for the first time I could go to the festival with someone at my side.

Maybe it was too soon to be thinking that way, but when he slipped his hand into mine, squeezing it slightly, I knew I wasn't imagining things.

"Yes, Willow," he said, a slight chuckle accompanying his words. "I still want to stay here." *With you.* He didn't say it, but I liked to think I could hear it in the tone of his voice. In the depth of his eyes. Even if he'd glamored them at my insistence.

"Okay." I turned my attention back to my fries, shoving a few in my mouth to hide my smile. "Just making sure," I mumbled under my breath.

We had some time to kill before we headed out to the farm for the festival. I needed to help Luna set up our table, but I already couldn't wait for everything.

There was no way I was holding back at the festival tonight. After all, pumpkin pie was my *favorite.* Luna was an amazing baker, but she'd never quite nailed pie, and Wendy—another member of our coven—made the best I'd ever tasted. Plus, topped with homemade whipped cream? I was in heaven. I practically moaned at the thought.

Damien gave me a strange look, and I flushed. "Sorry. Just thinking about pie." I gave a dreamy sigh.

"Pie?" His face scrunched up.

"You have *had* pie before, right?"

"Willow. I'm a demon. I wasn't born yesterday." He narrowed his eyes, stealing a fry from my basket.

"Mhm. Just wait until you taste it. It's the best pumpkin pie I've ever had." Popping another fry in my mouth, I couldn't resist it. "So good."

The idea of introducing all of my favorite foods to the man

sitting beside me warmed my insides. Showing him my town, my home—my life—it felt *good*.

He gave me a stare, his jaw tight as he stopped chewing.

Tilting my head back, I smiled up at the ceiling as I finished the rest of my fries. I hadn't considered how fun it might be to tease him. Sure, he had limited knowledge of human things—probably because he'd lived in the demon realm for over two hundred years—but his reaction was the fun part.

"So... where to next?"

damien

There were pumpkins everywhere.

Literally.

Willow had insisted we go back to her house and change before the evening's festivities. I'd pulled on a soft, dark gray henley and a flannel jacket with my jeans. The temperatures started to drop in the evening, and even if the cold didn't bother me much, I'd watched Willow shiver on the couch multiple times this week.

There was a reason that there was always a blanket handy next to us on the couch.

My mouth went dry when she walked out of her bedroom. Her body was wrapped in a long-sleeved pumpkin orange (because of course it was) dress that seemed to accentuate every curve, making her look like the embodiment of sin.

She was always beautiful, but this was—*wow*. The tan boots she'd pulled on gave her a few extra inches, making me that much closer to her mouth, and—

There was something seriously wrong with me.

A fuck-ton of pumpkins surrounded me, but all I could think about was her lips. Soft, pink, and ever so sweet. I wondered what she'd taste like. If the taste of pumpkin would overpower the vanilla-and-coffee scent that always followed her around.

I'd never wondered what anyone *tasted like* before, but I couldn't get it out of my mind.

Her eyes lit up as soon as she stepped out of her car. Even though I'd told her I knew how to drive—how uncivilized did she think we demons were, anyway?—she insisted on it.

I'd let her do it a thousand times, though, just to see that look on her face again.

"I have to go help Luna set up," Willow said. "But then I'm all yours."

Yours. Why did I like the way that word slipped off her tongue? Especially when it set off my *instincts*, the ones that wanted *everything*.

"Okay." My voice was thick, and I tried to push the thought away as I followed her through the crowd, towards the blonde girl setting up a tented stall.

Luna's cookies, individually wrapped in cute little bags with ghost prints, filled one table, while the other boasted a drink station.

"And you do this every year?" I asked, not sure what to do as I watched Willow stir her hot chocolate.

Luna gave me a smile, and I tried not to grimace as her powers hit my senses. It was insane to me that no one else could feel it. All of that magical potential, and she baked *cookies* for a living.

"Yep. Ever since we opened the shop." Happiness radiated off of her, which further cemented just how much she loved her job.

And you're going to ruin that for her, my brain took the time to remind me.

But Willow... She didn't have the same spark in her eye that

Luna did. I could tell she loved her sister, and loved the shop, but it wasn't her *passion*.

"I'm done!" She said, popping back up at my side. "Luna, you don't mind if we take off, right?"

The smell of chocolate and sweets wafted over to where I was standing.

Her sister shook her head. "Nah, go ahead. Cait's coming to keep me company, anyway."

I thought Willow had mentioned her to me—their cousin. Was she the one who wanted to hex her ex?

"Great." Willow turned back to me with a smile. "What should we do first?"

I cleared my throat. "This is your thing. Why don't you pick?"

My witch bit her lip, looking around at the festival. She'd really undersold the event when she'd told me about it earlier. I expected a few food stalls and some low-key small town attractions, but this place looked like a big carnival. There were tons of games set up and even some small rides they'd brought in.

I recognized one of them: the Spider. I'd been on that before. It'd almost made me throw up, so I had no desire to do it again. Really, I was content just following her around. I'd gladly let her eat her pie, while possibly feeding me copious amounts of sugar. I wasn't sure if I'd ever have another opportunity like this, after all. To be normal. To feel like a human and not a demon who wasn't even close to being in the middle of his life.

"Well... Do you want to take a ride?" Willow asked, forcing me out of my stupor.

I turned my attention back to her eyes. If I kept looking at her lips, I was going to do something stupid.

Like kiss her.

"What?"

She pointed at the little red tractor pulling a cart with an open back full of hay bales. "It's practically tradition."

I raised an eyebrow. "That doesn't look very comfortable."

My witch giggled. "Maybe not, but you drink a cup of hot cider and cuddle up under a blanket, so it's not so bad. Plus, the view is amazing."

I looked around, trying to see it through her eyes. Strings of lights adorned the farm, adding a touch of magic that perfectly complemented the changing leaves and the sunset in the background.

The world was a blanket of orange, and she was at the center.

"It is," I murmured in agreement. It was nice, but she was the most beautiful thing here.

Willow laced her fingers through my hand, beaming up at me. I loved her smile. It made me wonder what lengths I would go to earn it, over and over again.

"Come on, try it!" Willow said, offering me up a forkful of pie. "I promise, it's *to die* for."

I raised an eyebrow. "Really?"

She pouted. "Just try it. Please? For me?"

"Okay," I agreed, bending down to her level. I couldn't say no when she looked at me with that face, anyway. "Feed it to me."

Willow's cheeks pinked as she held up the fork to my mouth, and I held her eye contact as I slowly took the bite off the fork.

"Mmm." I licked my lips. I hadn't known quite what to

expect, but the texture was incredible, and the whipped topping must have been homemade, because it was rich and delicious.

It could rival a feast in the Demon King's palace.

"You have a bit of—" She giggled, pointing at my upper lip.

"What?"

"—Whipped cream. Right there."

Her thumb brushed over the top of my lip, capturing the bit of cream.

"Oh." I looked away, clearing my throat. "Thank you."

She was staring at her thumb, and I bent down, licking it off with my tongue.

"Damien!" Willow turned pink. "You can't just do that here. What if someone sees us?"

And what if they do, little witch?

A little scowl formed on her face. *Do you want people to know who you are? What if something happens to you again?*

Then it's a good thing I have a fearsome witch on my side this time, isn't it? I wove my fingers back through hers, kissing her knuckles. *Besides, look around. Everyone is enjoying themselves, too.*

No one was paying any attention to us. All around us, there were families laughing, the parents holding their kids' hands with blissful smiles on their faces as they ate bucketfuls of sugar. Older couples quietly strolled along as they likely reminisced about the past. Even the teens looked like they were enjoying themselves, playing the carnival games, determined to win.

I could see the Witches' Brew booth from here. Luna was flitting around, helping customers as she handed out bags of cookies and cups of hot chocolate. Frowning, I turned to Willow, about to ask if we should help, when—

"Willow?" A voice called, and a female, dressed in all black, rushed to catch up with us. "Who's your friend?"

"Oh." My witch peeked over at me. "This is Damien. My..." she trailed off, looking at me. I hated how she didn't have a label for me.

But what was I? I'd known her for a week and a half, and most of that, I'd been stuck as a cat for. A fact that never failed to raise my hackles. *Roommate? Friend?* Something more? I desperately wanted to know how she was going to answer it.

I caught her eye, answering it when she failed to. "Friend," I confirmed. I liked when she'd called me that before.

"Damien, this is Cait. She's my cousin."

The orange-haired witch stuck out her hand for me to shake it. "It's nice to meet you," she beamed. I'd never met a witch quite like her before. She had a nose ring and beautiful tattoos that went up the sides of her arms, and her tights looked like snakes.

"Cousins, huh?" If I looked really closely between the two of them, I could see the similarities. They had the same shape of their nose and structure to their jaw. But her cousin had dyed her hair, and her eyes were nothing like the bright green of Willow's—that reminded me of Granny Smith apples.

"Yup. Our moms were sisters." Cait gave me a warm smile.

"We're in the same coven," Willow added as her cousin threw an arm around her shoulder, hugging Willow tight.

"Ah," I said, nodding. "Of course."

It was a sobering reminder—these people would be in Willow's life forever.

And me? Maybe we'd have a month. One *good* month. I wanted to make sure it counted.

"Come on," Willow said, tugging my hand. "Let's go find pumpkins."

We said our goodbyes to her cousin, and I completely

forgot about mentioning helping Luna as she pulled me toward the pumpkin patch.

I frowned, looking at a sea of endless pumpkins. "What exactly am I looking for? I've never exactly done this before."

She looked surprised for a moment before smoothing her expression out, bending down to look at the orange squash at her feet. "You want one that's a good shape, medium to large size, and a smooth surface." Willow pointed out a few examples on the ground. "Though I suppose it all depends on what you want to carve into it, anyway." She bit her lip, and I couldn't help but stare at her teeth digging into those sweet, pink lips.

I blinked away the thought of what it would be like to do that to her.

"Was I supposed to think of something before this?" Because I definitely hadn't.

"Oh. Well. I suppose not." Willow brushed her hands on the skirt of her dress before standing up, leaning against me. "But you will... carve one with me, right?" Her eyes were pleading, practically begging. But she didn't have to ask.

"Of course," I chuckled. "Anything you want, Wil." Wrapping an arm around her waist, I pulled her in tighter to me, inhaling the smell of her sweetness. I couldn't get enough of it.

"Oh!" she squealed, pulling away from me. "I found them!" She rushed farther down the row, where two pumpkins were sitting side by side. They were almost equal in color and shape, despite one being slightly smaller than the other. "What do you think?" She looked up at me, and I nodded.

"Perfect." But I wasn't talking about the pumpkins.

Hefting them into my arms, I took them over to the weigh station so Willow could pay for them before depositing them in the car.

On our way back, Willow stopped at a few food booths,

continuing to feed me different sweets. I'd lost how many forms of pumpkin I'd tried. Fudge, bread, muffins, scones...

"How are you still eating?" I asked her, watching her plop another bite of pumpkin spice cake in her mouth.

She stopped chewing to stare at me. "I have a bottomless stomach for sweets." Willow's voice was so matter-of-fact. "Obviously."

I wiped a smudge of frosting from the corner of her lip before she handed me a small bag of candy.

"What is this?"

Picking one out, I held up the strange multicolored candy —yellow, orange, and white in a triangle shape.

She giggled. "It's candy corn. Try it. It's one of my favorites." *Corn?* I made a skeptical face before popping it into my mouth.

Sweet. I made a face. It tasted like frosting and sugar, all rolled into one.

"What?" She laughed. "You don't like it?"

"It's too sweet. Are you sure you aren't just eating pure sugar?"

Willow stuck her tongue out at me, grabbing a few pieces from my bag. "More for me, thank you."

I didn't mind at all as she finished it, entranced by watching her happily munch on the candy.

"Should we go through the maze now?" She asked, looking towards the stacks of straw bales stacked on top of each other.

We promptly deposited our food wrappers in the trash before she dragged me over to it.

The witch working the front handed us a map of the maze, so we could apparently find our way out of it. I stared at the diagram, showing the view from above. They'd made the damn thing the shape of a jack-o'-lantern, complete with the eyes and mouth in the middle.

"One year, they made it so hard that old Granny Crowley couldn't figure out how to get out of it. They had to send in a search party," she giggled.

"It's a pumpkin," I stated plainly.

"Last year it was a ghost." She pretended to look contemplative. "Should I see if next year they'll make it a cat?"

I rolled my eyes, pulling her into the opening of the maze. "Let's do this."

But when I turned around, she couldn't see the ghost of a smile that spread over my lips.

How much straw could be in one fucking place? Hell. This place was *actual* hell. We'd been going through it for fifteen minutes already, but it felt like hours. The tall walls of straw made me feel trapped, like I couldn't get out—even though I knew it would only take a moment, one use of my power to get out.

Letting my shadows curl through my fingers, I breathed out, calming down slightly.

I turned around to ask my witch a question, but she wasn't behind me.

"Willow?" I spun around. Where'd she go? "Willow!" I shouted, backtracking slightly, checking the other branches of the path before going back to where we hadn't walked yet.

"Fuck," I cursed, rubbing my forehead.

How had I managed to lose her?

This place was claustrophobic, and despite the map, I still felt completely turned around.

"Got you!" She said, popping up behind me.

"Willow. For fuck's sake. Don't do that." I rubbed my forehead.

"What?" She frowned.

"I thought—" *You were lost. That something had happened to you.* "Never mind." I shook my head.

96

"I was just—" Willow started, moving towards me, but there was a patch of mud on the ground in between us, and her foot slipped, launching her forward.

As she stumbled, I quickly reached out and wrapped my arms around her waist to prevent her from falling.

"Oh." Willow breathed, and I was vividly aware of the fact that the hay bales hid us from view, secluded in the maze.

She smelled so sweet; I had to stop myself from leaning over to find the source of the scent. Was it her shampoo? Or just something uniquely her?

Fuck.

"Little witch..." I groaned.

I was losing control.

If I wasn't careful, I was going to take her.

My lips parted, and the slightest breath of air escaped them as I stared at his face. Into those dark eyes, which I never failed to get lost in. No matter if they were red or deep chocolate brown, there was something so captivating about them. About him, really.

I let my gaze linger down to his lips.

There was no mistaking the way he did the same.

We were so close together, barely an inch left between our bodies, and I was struck with the sudden realization that I *wanted* him. More than I ever could have imagined.

Maybe I shouldn't have—he was a demon, after all, and my whole life I'd been taught to stay away from them—but I couldn't help it anymore.

Not when I'd spent the entire day in his presence, and he'd let me drag him wherever I'd wanted to go. When we'd been sitting together on the hayride, our thighs touching, sharing the same blanket... I wondered, *was he feeling the same way?*

"Willow," his voice rasped out. "Don't look at me like that."

"Like what?" Mine was hardly a whisper against the wind, but I hadn't needed to say it at all.

My tongue ran over my lips, moistening them as we stared at each other. If we moved just a fraction of an inch, we'd be kissing. All I had to do was lean up, and—

"Like you want me to kiss you."

His hand tightened on my waist, keeping me pinned firmly to him. The other spread across my back, and the heat from his palm was practically burning me, but I didn't want it to stop.

"But..." I looked up at him through my eyelashes. "What if I do?"

"Little witch..." He warned, a pained expression forming over his features, even as I gripped his jacket tighter. "I don't think you know what you're getting yourself into."

I did. But... *I don't care.* The realization struck me, hard and fast. I didn't care what I got into with this man, this demon, as long as he kissed me.

"Kiss me," I whispered. "Please."

He exhaled roughly before that hand holding my back threaded through my hair, and he bent down and—Damien's lips were on mine.

Soft, like he was gauging my response. Making sure I was okay with it. Wrapping my hands around his neck, I curled my fingers into his hair, tugging him down more forcefully against my mouth.

The first stroke of his tongue against mine had me gasping. The sudden surety—the rightness I felt—I'd never felt like this kissing *anyone* before.

Magic, my brain wanted to say. But I knew magic, and this was nothing like my powers.

Not when every movement of his tongue in my mouth, every press of his lips against mine had me dizzy, my mind blurring.

I wanted *more.*

I wanted him to kiss me like this forever.

Sighing into his mouth, I wrapped my arms around his neck.

That was all the invitation he needed to pick me up, spinning me around to pin me against the straw bales as he explored my mouth with his tongue, not letting go.

"Fuck, Willow," he murmured, awe in his voice as his eyes traced over every inch of my face. Lingering, memorizing. I tugged on the back of his hair, pulling his mouth back to mine.

Bringing our lips together. Now that I'd felt it, I didn't want to stop.

By the time we made it out of the maze, the sun was gone from the sky.

"Look!" They'd fully decked the barn out for the festival, the string of lights on the ceiling illuminating the dance floor. "It's beautiful." I emitted a dreamy sigh.

I'd always dreamed of having a wedding like this one day. If I met the right person. Lately, that had seemed less and less likely. Except...

The man by my side was making me think of things like that again. Which I couldn't afford to do. He'd only said he'd stay for a month. I couldn't expect a lifetime from a demon, of all people.

He wasn't from here. Didn't belong in Pleasant Grove. I let loose a deep sigh.

Damien rubbed his thumb over the crease in between my brows. "What are you thinking, little witch?"

I shook my head. "Nothing." Forcing a smile on my face, I refocused my attention on the barn. "It doesn't matter."

He looked skeptical, but I ignored that. "Do you want to get a drink? They have pumpkin beer."

Damien groaned. "You and pumpkin. Is there anything in the flavor that you don't like?"

"Nope!" I beamed. "I even have pumpkin cupcake scented body wash."

Grumbling under his breath, he said something that I was pretty sure sounded like, *Of course you do.* But I couldn't be sure.

Still, I pulled him over to the bar, ordering a beer for him and a pumpkin hard cider for me.

Damien's eyes trailed over the room as he sipped his drink. He made a face after swallowing. "That is... truly something."

I laughed. "It's okay if you don't like it. I won't be offended if you don't finish it."

He grunted, taking another sip.

My eyes tracked the movement as his tongue slid over his bottom lip, catching the extra drops of liquid. I could practically feel my body heating as I thought about that kiss earlier —feeling his tongue against mine. Wondering what else it could do.

You're losing it, Willow, I told myself, awkwardly avoiding eye contact as I chugged my cider. I should have picked something with a higher alcohol content—maybe it would have given me the courage to be more bold.

Instead, I was standing and watching the couples on the dance floor twirling their partners in their arms. They were doing some sort of upbeat, country two-step dance I ought to have known by now. I wasn't much for dancing, though. Maybe I just hadn't found the right partner.

"Come here," Damien whispered, holding his hand out to me.

I took it, surprised when he spun me into his arms.

"Oh, you have moves, do you?" Maybe part of me was just surprised he knew how to dance. Especially as he spun me around, his feet moving faster than my eyes could seem to keep up with.

"It's the demon realm, not hell," he said, his deep voice rough against my ear. "I learned how to dance when I was young." Why did that make him even more endearing?

He shut his eyes, a warm smile curling on his lips. "My mother loved to dance."

"Damien..." I murmured. That was the sweetest thing he'd ever said. "What happened to her?" I'd lost my own parents, but hearing him talk about her in the past tense made my heart ache.

He shook his head. "My father... the palace... even with all the guards, it wasn't the safest place for her." A distant look filled his eyes, like he was thinking about the past. "She died protecting me."

I knew what it was like—losing a parent—but not like that. "Mine passed in a boating accident," I said in a whisper. "I'm sorry you had to go through that alone."

His eyes connected with mine, and the pain evident in them... It made me want to kiss him again, just to take it away for a little while. Or maybe give him a hug. I wasn't sure which one. But given that we were in the middle of a crowded dance floor, I just kept letting him lead me.

"It's been a long time." His grip on my back tightened. "It doesn't hurt as much anymore."

I rested my head on his shoulder. "That pain... It never really leaves you, though."

"No," he agreed. "It doesn't."

We were quiet for awhile after that, just losing ourselves in the music's flow.

"Can I ask what happened to them?" Damien's voice was quiet, resigned. Like he thought I wouldn't answer.

"I don't talk about it much," I said, honestly. "Most people in town know what happened, and my coven, well... You're the first person who's asked about them in a long time." I fiddled with his shirt with my hand that wasn't still holding onto his. "They've been gone for years. I still miss them, of course, but I stopped crying ages ago. I had to be strong for Luna. Keep it together for her."

"How old were you?" He murmured.

"21. I was in college when I got a call. There was a freak accident. And Luna, she... She'd barely graduated high school."

He rubbed my back. "So you came back?"

I nodded. "So I came back. Finished a semester early, got my degree, and then kept our house from falling apart as Luna went to pastry school. She knew what she wanted and I..." Didn't. Hadn't had a dream.

"Did everything for your sister."

"Yup."

He made a noise of agreement. "I know what that's like. To feel you've given up your life for your sibling."

"It's not that I don't think it was worth it. I love Luna. I love working together, the business we've grown. The Witches' Brew is my baby as much as it is hers. It's just..."

"Not your dream."

I looked up at him. "Yeah," I whispered. "It's not my dream."

He cleared his throat. "So what is?"

"You know, I think I'm still figuring it out."

"Me too."

I laughed. "What, two hundred and eighty-seven years wasn't enough to figure out what you wanted to do with your life?"

Damien brushed a hair behind my ear. "It didn't feel like much of a life until I met you."

Our eyes connected again, and this time—I held his gaze. Drank it in. Reveled in it.

Knew that something about it was going to change my life.

Maybe in all the ways I'd always dreamed it would.

I was in more trouble than I'd thought. I was letting myself get distracted with pumpkin patches and dances and the intoxicating presence of Willow. Thinking that maybe this could last. That there was some way I could make it work.

Like I wasn't a demon with responsibilities that didn't involve getting entangled with a witch.

But that *kiss*.

I hadn't been planning on kissing her. I was trying so fucking hard to be good. To not tarnish her sunshine with my darkness. But I couldn't help it. When she'd looked up at me with those big green eyes—I'd lost any semblance of self control.

Looking over at the passenger seat, I watched Willow sleep, her head turned towards me even with her eyes closed.

I wanted this. Wanted her. But I couldn't have her.

"Fuck," I muttered, turning back to stare at the house. It was a miracle she'd let me drive home. I'd had to prove to her that I did, in fact, have a driver's license—even though it had been faked by the demon realm, since I wasn't exactly a human with real ID—and that I could drive her car before she relented.

But she'd been exhausted. After hours of swaying on the dance floor, her eyes had been closing on their own.

And now, I couldn't bring myself to wake her up. So instead I was staring at her, tracing the lines of her face with my eyes.

But I couldn't help myself, and I reached out, brushing over her cheekbone with my thumb.

"Hmm?" Willow gave a small groan as she stirred from her nap.

"We're here," I said, looking up at her house.

"Oh." My witch yawned, stretching out her arms. "Thanks again for driving."

"No problem." I cleared my throat, avoiding looking at her dress, or the way it had ridden up, exposing more of her thighs.

My mouth went dry.

"We should go inside," I whispered.

"Yeah." Her voice was quiet, low. "We should."

Padding into her guest bathroom, I looked at myself in the mirror.

You need to get it together, Damien, I scolded myself. *She's not yours to touch.*

But our kiss was replaying in my mind.

The way her soft, smooth lips moved over mine. The way she'd sighed so sweetly into my mouth. How she tasted so fucking good. I wanted more.

But—no.

Stripping off my clothes, I stayed in my boxers, leaving the rest folded neatly on the counter.

When I'd come out, Willow had left a pillow and blanket on the couch. It was strange to think that this was only our first night sleeping under the same roof with me in this form. That every other night, I'd slept on her feet.

I chuckled, looking at the pile of bedding. *The couch.*

Because even if she'd kissed me back—I was still a stranger. This wasn't serious. It wasn't like she was going to invite me to her bed.

Not again. Not yet, at least.

But...

Turning back into my cat form, I waited until she'd turned her lights off and gone to sleep, and then I slipped into her room, curling up at her feet.

Where I could protect her—my small, little witch—from harm.

THIRTEEN

I woke up in a panic. There was something on top of me, something warm, and—I kicked, trying to get it off of me.

"Willow!" A smooth, rich, *angry* voice grit out. Oh no.

"Damien?" I peeked over the bed and instantly regretted it.

"What the *fuck* was that for?"

"I... I can't..." I blinked.

He was naked. Completely nude, and gloriously bare, and —"I told you to sleep on the couch!" I practically yelled. "And can you put some clothes on, *please?*"

I was trying not to stare. Luckily, it was dark, and I could only see the outline of his chest and... other regions. There was no mistaking *that.*

Damien's voice was full of humor. "Why, like what you see?"

I threw a pillow at his face. "No!" *Yes.* I was glad it was dark enough in here to hide the flush on my face.

Damien placed the pillow over the lower half of his body, and I swallowed roughly. I was trying not to think about the shape of it. He was a large male, and even the impressive size of his package... *Woah.*

This was not good for my health.

"Why didn't this happen before?"

"Because I wasn't asleep when I transformed before." He narrowed his eyes at me. "And I certainly didn't expect to be kicked off the bed while I was sleeping."

"You were *supposed* to be on the couch."

"Maybe I don't like the couch," he huffed, a lock of dark hair falling onto his forehead. "Besides, perhaps I just wanted to keep an eye on you."

"To what? Make sure I don't curse you too?" I rolled my eyes. "You can relax, Damien. I'm not going to do anything to you."

He ground his teeth. "Maybe I'm not worried about myself."

I blinked. *Me?* He was worried about... *me?* "*Why?*" I asked, nothing more than a whisper in the night.

"There are worse things out there than me, little witch. Things you can't even imagine."

There was more he wasn't saying—it was obvious in his tone, in the fear that crept into his voice. Was that why he'd been so freaked out when I'd lost him in the maze?

What could such a powerful demon like him be afraid of?

I frowned. "Nothing's going to happen to me. This is Pleasant Grove." The name was fitting for our town. It was a happy, friendly place. *Pleasant.* "Not here. Our wards and spells are exceptional."

Except... if they were so good, how did Damien get here in the first place? They should have warded off other magical species as much as they did non-magical beings. If a regular human *did* somehow end up in our town, then they would see whatever their brain would make them believe.

Normally, it was people who thought we were putting on a show, living some recreation of a witch town in the 1700s.

But there was a reason I'd never seen a demon before him. They had taught us they were bad. To fear them.

Yet I knew Damien wasn't like that. He'd given me little peeks into his life, his mind—his heart. He wasn't a bad person. Nor was he out here trying to get me to sign over my soul to him, or agree to some other contract.

And then... there was the way he'd kissed me.

So softly, and then with such intensity.

There'd been no mistaking the way he wanted me. Right? I'd felt it when he'd had me pinned up against the straw. Except we'd come home, and he'd... stayed away from me. Waited until I fell asleep to come in here—in cat form—and do the same.

So he might have wanted me, but he didn't want to act on those impulses.

Which was worse?

"Damien..." I breathed, but I didn't know what to ask. What to say.

I just turned over, facing the other wall. "I'm going back to sleep," I murmured, not looking back at him as I heard him clamber up off of the floor.

As he padded away into the other room.

There was one thing I knew for sure: Damien might not have been a dangerous demon, but he was dangerous for my heart.

Because I *wanted* him.

Despite my best efforts, I couldn't get back to sleep, and the rest of the night was spent tossing and turning. As the first light of dawn appeared, I quickly showered and dressed before rushing out of the house.

Maybe I didn't know what was going on with Damien, why

I was feeling this way, but it was okay—I had my sister, and she always had good advice for me. Sometimes I forgot I was the older sister, because she seemed wise beyond her years. Damn precognition skills.

It was a windy, rainy day, so I took my car, pulling into a spot right off Main Street and bundling my raincoat tighter to me as I walked to the bakery.

The moment I stepped inside, I could hear the familiar sound of my sister's mixing bowl clattering against the counter. She normally beat me here since she rented out the apartment overtop of the bakery.

She'd piled her blonde hair high in a bun, with a pretty pink scrunchie holding it all together, matching her overall dress and turtleneck perfectly.

One of these days, I was going to find it in me to be annoyed that she always looked this cute so early in the morning. It had taken all of my energy to throw on a pair of jeans

"Mmm. Smells good in here." It always did, without fail.

"I hope so," she smiled. "I made doughnuts."

My mouth watered. "Doughnuts? What's the special occasion?" I was always trying to get her to add them to the regular menu, but Luna insisted they were too much work. Despite that, our customers loved them.

"No special occasion," she shrugged. "I just felt like it."

Using my magic, I moved my hand like I was going to levitate one out of the pan, but she smacked my hand away. "Later. They're still too warm. Let the icing set." She raised an eyebrow at me. "Why are you here so early this morning, anyway?"

Damn, I thought as I braided my hair back and tied my apron around my waist. *Busted.*

"No reason," I said, busying myself with prep for the day. "I was awake, so I thought I'd come spend time with my sister."

"Mmm. *Sure.*" She said it like she didn't believe me, but at least most of that was true. I *did* want to spend time with her.

"Yup," I said, popping the *p* as I got everything out to make myself a coffee.

"So, how's your cat?" Luna asked, looking up from her bowl of dough she was working on.

"He, uh... Ran away?" I could already feel my cheeks pinking, thinking about Damien and how glad I was that he *wasn't* a cat.

My sister gave me a knowing smile. "Sure. And that has nothing to do with your new mystery man, hm?"

I ignored her question, instead voicing one that had been bouncing around my mind all morning. Or maybe it had been longer than that, something I didn't want to admit. "Luna, I... Do you believe in fate? In destiny?"

Luna blinked. "Where is this coming from?" She moved over to the mixer, where she was mixing up more frosting.

I shook my head. "No reason. Just..." I sighed.

How did I explain to her how I was feeling? Or maybe that was the problem itself—that I didn't want to put these thoughts into words. To verbalize my fears and hopes, because then they'd be real.

"I believe the Goddess gives us the paths we can follow, but the rest is up to us."

Biting my lip, I turned to face my sister fully. "But like... Twin Flames, Kindred Spirits, *Soul Mates.* That stuff. Do you believe there's someone out there who you're fated to be with? To fall in love with?"

She tilted her head. "You've always told me not to look into your future. That you didn't want to know. But now..." Luna raised an eyebrow.

"No!" I exclaimed a little too quickly, the question clear in her face. "I still don't want to know." My voice was barely audible as I lowered it to a murmur. "I was just wondering."

Luna turned off the mixer, setting the bowl on the counter in between the two of us, and leveled a stare at me. "Willow, what are you really asking me?"

"When Mom met Dad, she *knew*, right? Do you think that's possible?"

She blinked and then nodded her head. "I think *anything's* possible, Willow." Luna moved the spoon in her frosting bowl with her magic. "Especially in a world where magic exists."

Maybe she was right. Nevertheless, that didn't explain why these thoughts were running through my head.

Even if it was real, it wasn't *Damien*. It couldn't be. He was an immortal demon prince, and I was just a witch.

"Hm." I swiped a finger through the rim of the bowl of frosting, getting a glob of the cream cheese mixture she'd made. "Yum. My favorite."

"Probably why I make it so much," Luna said with a smile. "There's a fresh batch of spice cake cupcakes to frost."

"You're the best sister ever." I wrapped my arms around her, pulling her into a tight hug.

"And *you* still owe me that bar date soon. I bought a new dress that I'm dying to wear out." She poked me in the arm.

"Okay," I agreed. Because we both deserved to have fun. And maybe it was time I finally *lived* my life, like she kept telling me. And maybe just a small piece of that had to do with Damien. The man who had been sleeping on my couch when I snuck out. "This weekend?"

"You're on. And not just because Friday is *Ghoul's* night at the bar." She wiggled her eyebrows.

"Attire?"

"Spooky. Naturally."

Gods, I loved Halloween time in Pleasant Grove. The way

everyone got so into it, with themed nights and decor. Somehow we stretched All Hallows' Eve into an entire month of festivities.

"I'll be there."

"Where are you going?" Damien asked, leaning against the doorframe as I attempted to zip up my dress. It was Friday night, Luna and I's big night out at The Enchanted Cauldron.

I turned to look at him, and my mouth dropped open.

Abs. Muscles. Towel around his waist.

Oh, Goddess.

My mouth went dry. I'd seen him shirtless before, even if it was in the cover of darkness and *mostly* just an outline of the ridges to his body. But this was... I shut my eyes.

"Did I adopt a demon, or a damn God?" I muttered under my breath, eyes still focused on his muscles. Those abs I wanted to trace my tongue over—multiple times, if I had my way. Especially after that kiss last week. It wasn't enough—I wanted more.

No being should be allowed to look like *that*. Especially when I was trying so hard to be good. There was a part of me that felt like a sex-crazed beast every time I saw him. One look from him was all it took, and I was wet. *Dripping*. It was unfair, really.

But he was basically my roommate, my *friend*, and he was leaving. He'd only promised me a month, and how much of that did I even have left?

But I couldn't ask him to stay.

Sure, we'd settled into some sort of normal routine over the last week. I'd go to work, stay at the bakery until the late afternoon before coming home and making dinner.

Damien—well, who knew what Damien did during the day.

But at night, we'd sit on the couch, a cushion between us, watching whatever Halloween movie was on the TV.

I still wasn't sure what to make out of my unexpected houseguest in a lot of ways, after all. Especially after he'd kissed me.

But nothing else had happened.

Damien hadn't kissed me again. We'd barely even touched since coming home from the festival. He hadn't made another move.

Sometimes, when he was looking at me, I'd catch his gaze dropping to my lips. Or the heat in his eyes.

Yet the complete rest of this week we just... hadn't talked about it. I was tired of dancing around the subject. Pretending there wasn't some heat between us that I couldn't explain.

"Out," I said with a huff, giving up on the zipper. It might have been a themed night, but I still wanted to look good. *Feel* good. For no one else but myself. Definitely not for the man who currently stood behind me.

"Here," he murmured, coming up behind me. "Let me."

Our eyes connected in the mirror as he slowly zipped up my dress, his breath ghosting on the back of my neck. The whole encounter probably took only seconds, but it felt private —intimate—and I didn't know what to make of that.

"Um." I smoothed my hands over the tight black dress. "Thank you."

His voice was rough. "Of course."

Looping my dangly ghost earrings through my ears, I looked over my appearance. It was casually spooky for sure, but I felt cute. I'd add my favorite hat and a pair of heels and call it good.

Damien leaned against the door frame. "Should I be worried about where you're going dressed like that?"

My eyes lifted in the mirror to his. "The bar. Luna wanted to go out." I bit my lip. "Why? Worried someone else is going to sweep me off my feet?"

The way his eyes lit up... Maybe that was exactly what he'd been worried about. And for some reason, I liked that I'd riled him up with just the one comment.

"I'm going with you," he said, his tone offering no room for argument.

I raised an eyebrow at his still naked body.

Maybe some clothes first?

He dressed in a flash—literally, with one snap of his fingers, and he was in a button-up shirt and a pair of slacks. One day, I needed to ask him how he did that. Where he stored his belongings that he could just retrieve them without blinking an eye.

I pondered that for a while, trying to ignore the truth bouncing around in my brain.

Somehow, he was even more handsome in dress clothes than just in the towel.

My eyes flickered over to Damien, who was sitting at the bar as my sister and I danced.

Maybe it was a little *too* on the nose to play *The Monster Mash* during Ghoul's Night, but it was fitting.

"You know... He's *hot!*" Luna shouted over the music. "Why don't you see where that goes?"

I shook my head. "He's not here forever. We're just friends! Roommates!" I hated that thought. *It's just temporary.* "And I... don't want to start something that will end." I hadn't realized that was how I felt until I uttered the words, but maybe that was why I'd let the wall form between us this last week. Sure, he had stayed, but for how long?

Distancing myself was safe.

Kissing him again... That was not.

"Okay, but the way he's watching you? Damn." She fanned herself.

I was pretty sure she had some inkling of who he *was*, especially after her comment earlier this week at the coffee shop, but I wondered if she knew the full story. That he was the cat she'd let brush up against her legs just a few days ago. That he was living under my roof.

Sleeping curled up on the edge of my bed every night, even though I'd find him back on the couch every morning. Like he didn't want me to find out.

"Luna, I should probably tell you—" I started, getting interrupted by the music changing. The crowd cheered around us.

"You just need to let loose, Willow! Get *laid!*" My sister said the last word with a singsong voice, and my body flushed.

"I... *Luna.*" I groaned, even as we moved to the beat.

"What?" She frowned, giving me a little shrug as she shimmied on the floor. "I can't have my older sister trying to take care of me forever. You have to live your own life, too, Wil."

My own life... My eyes wandered up, connecting with Damien's, who was still sitting at the bar, sipping his drink. Watching me dance.

But the heat in his eyes... I wasn't mistaking it this time. Definitely not.

"Do you want to dance?"

117

The words were ones I wanted to hear—but they weren't from the right person.

I turned around, and there was Simon from the library, his auburn hair combed back, and a bowtie that looked like a bat tied around his neck.

"Oh, I..." I looked back to the bar, but Damien was gone, his empty drink sitting on the counter. "I actually came here with someone. Sorry." I winced involuntarily.

"Yeah," my demon agreed, pulling my back flush against his chest. "With me."

I turned my head to look up at him, my cheeks heating at the determination I saw there.

You're beautiful. The words I should have said to Willow earlier, when I saw her standing in her bathroom, the black dress showing off the creamy smooth skin of her back. Instead, I'd practically forced her to bring me along tonight.

Dammit. How hard was it to say the words?

All week, I'd had them on the tip of my tongue.

But everything faded away whenever she was around.

The light brown strands of her hair caught the light as she danced with Luna, and I scowled at the thought of someone else touching her. I shouldn't have been this possessive, but watching her sway her hips, thinking about anyone else having what was *mine*...

It was enough to make my lips curl over my teeth.

"Fuck," I muttered to myself as I watched the two of them dance.

"Can I get you another one, sir?" The bartender asked me, and I shook my head.

I'd been nursing the same one all night, and I had no plans

of getting drunk. There was no way I'd risk something happening to Willow—or her sister.

I took another sip as the two girls danced. They'd been playing popular Halloween songs all night. Some I recognized, and others I had never heard before. While I wasn't well versed in a lot of human culture—especially with their holidays—I'd spent my fair share of time while on this mission in bars. That, at least, wasn't all that different from the demon realm.

And it was the reason I didn't take my eyes off of them. Not for a second.

Part of me had hoped to find the girl I was looking for in one, but that had only led to me being cursed. The damn witch who took one look at me, talking to her sister, and decided I was bad news. Well, I deserved that.

Especially when the girl I'd been searching for was currently by Willow's side. She'd been here all along, like destiny was just waiting for me to find both of them.

Gods. Her sister.

How was I going to explain everything to her? I rubbed my thumb over the top of my glass. I'd been doing so good all week, trying to build a relationship with her. Getting to know *her*.

I watched her human movies and then she told me about her past. What growing up here was like. About her relationship with her coven and her sister. How she'd thought about moving somewhere else after college. I couldn't listen to her talk about the human boys she'd been with, not without my veins filling with rage. The jealousy was almost suffocating, the way it hit me out of nowhere.

There was no prying my eyes away from her.

The redheaded boy from the library was moving closer to my witch, making my hair practically stand up on my arms. My body sang for me to defend her, to claim her publicly.

To make it known that she was *mine.*

I was out of my chair before I knew what I was doing, pulling Willow's body into mine. Covering her in my scent.

Her head tilted back to look at me, and I watched as her cheeks pinked. Fuck, I liked that. How had I gone this whole week without touching her? Without taking her lips in mine again?

"She's here with me," I repeated, as the young wizard looked between the two of us.

"I'm sorry, Willow." He looked embarrassed. "I didn't know you were seeing anyone."

"We're just..." My witch looked up at me as she said, "It's still new." She offered him a small shrug.

"Hey, no worries." He gave a sad smile before turning around, going to the other side of the packed dance floor.

"Do you want to get a drink?" I murmured into her ear, my lips brushing against her neck as I pulled away.

She nodded, mumbling, "Mhm," in response. Even the tips of her ears were a little pink as she slipped her hand into mine and led me back across the room.

Willow slid onto a barstool, her hand staying intertwined in mine even as I took the one next to her. Watching her, my eyes traced her flushed cheeks, her eyes twinkling as she ordered another drink. If only I could commit it to memory, so I'd never have to forget this moment. Or her.

Once she had the cocktail in her hands, she spun around to look at me, her eyes bright. "Hi."

"Hey," I practically grunted back.

I was still struggling with the possession I'd felt earlier, the need to claim her as mine in front of everyone. Her smell was in my nostrils, and I wanted it deeper. In my lungs, maybe. Burrowed underneath my skin. My innate nature was hard to deny.

"Sorry if this is boring for you," my witch frowned.

It wasn't. Not when I'd been unable to take my eyes off of her all fucking night.

"You could never bore me," I said. Fuck it all. I didn't like the distance we'd had in the past week, so maybe it was time for honesty. "Besides, this is... enlightening."

Watching her. Seeing how she let loose.

"Hm? Can demons get drunk, anyway?" Willow wondered out loud, sucking on the straw of her drink, her eyes wide as she watched me.

"Of course we can." I looked around the room. Luckily, no one was paying attention to us or her words, or else we could be in trouble.

Not because I was worried about something happening to me. The last thing I wanted was for someone to confront Willow about *me*. The idea that I could make problems for her just because of who I was... I didn't like that. But I was already here, being a selfish bastard, all because I couldn't seem to walk away from her—but I didn't want to affect her reputation.

Because it was clear, any time she was around other people, whether it was flitting around the bar or in her coffee shop, just how beloved she was.

I'd experienced nothing like this town in the demon realm. Not that there weren't communities or towns of our own—demons, living in their true forms, free to live their lives—but my life had been cold. Emotionless. Sometimes it felt almost meaningless. I'd lost my mom at a young age. My father... Well, the Demon King had his own set of worries, and it wasn't about me. No, that distinction went to my older brother. The *Heir*.

I scrubbed a hand over my face. She'd lost her parents, but she was still so kind, caring, and generous. In all my years, I'd never met a woman who enchanted me the way Willow did. I couldn't stop. Couldn't keep my eyes off of her, or my body from wanting to touch her. Wrap her soft brown curls around my fist and—

Willow's hand landed on my thigh, causing me to startle out of my thoughts.

"What?" My eyes flickered to the counter, to her finished drink. Mine was gone now too, meaning I had no more excuse to be a grumpy asshole tonight.

"Should we dance?" She held out her hand to me. The music had slowed—no longer one of those poppy hits she had been moving her hips to.

I thought about how good it had felt the other day— holding her in my arms, dancing with her. Even though I knew it was dangerous, that nothing good would come out of it, I couldn't say no. Couldn't bring myself to turn her down.

"Of course," I murmured, giving her my hand. It always amazed me how much smaller hers were than mine. How I could wrap my entire hand around hers. And yet, when she laced her fingers through mine, nothing had ever fit so perfectly.

Yes, my body screamed as my hand wrapped around her waist, pulling her in closer to me.

"You look beautiful tonight," I murmured against her ear, finally saying what I'd been dying to for hours.

"Thank you." She bobbed her head, a pretty blush spreading over her cheeks. "You clean up pretty nicely yourself."

I'd hardly noticed what I'd thrown on when she told me about her plans. I'd just focused on her bare back as I zipped up her dress, and the way it hugged her curves. So fucking perfect.

Begging to have my hands all over them.

A dark shadow caught my eye in the back of the bar. Some alarm bell went off inside my mind, that I should investigate— to see what was going on.

But then Willow wrapped her arms around me, and nothing else mattered.

Unlike at the festival, when I twirled and spun her around the room, in a dance of intricate steps, we just held each other, swaying to the music. I liked it too much.

Which was why I needed to come clean.

"Willow..." I sighed, opting for honesty. "I'm sorry for this week."

She looked confused. "Why? I thought we were having a good time." She tilted her head to the side. "Getting to know each other. You know."

"We were. And I liked it. Watching your human movies. Listening to your stories." Too much. I liked it way too much. "But I've been avoiding... *this*, and it's not fair to you." I swallowed roughly, fingers itching to dig into her skin. "To either of us."

"No," she agreed, "it's not."

"But..." I tightened my grip on her hip. Held her closer to my body. Let my breath brush against her ear, and watched the way she shuddered from it.

Her eyes were closed as she murmured a quiet, "But?"

"But I'm tired of holding back. Pretending I don't want you. Pretending I don't know what your mouth tastes like. Pretending I don't want to do it again."

Willow's eyes flew open, her hand on my shoulder moving to grip my jacket instead. "You do?"

My lips ghosted against her neck, the faintest press of a kiss to her perfect skin. "I do."

When I stared back down at her, there was a spellbound

look in her eyes. "Oh, good." She let loose a giggle. "Because I do as well."

I looked into her eyes. They were big, but not overly dilated. And she didn't seem drunk to me. Which meant...

She wanted me as badly as I wanted her.

"Should we go home?" Willow whispered, her eyes bright. "Because I really want to kiss you right now."

"Yes." And fuck, I liked the sound of that. *Home.* Her place felt more like home than anywhere I'd ever been before.

I was so close to losing control. To giving in to every thought, every desire.

What the hell were we still doing here?

"Will Luna be okay?" I asked, looking at her sister, currently chatting with another witch at the bar.

Willow nodded. "She's a big girl. She can take care of herself."

And before either of us could utter another word, her hand was in mine, and I was pulling her towards the door.

"Willow." His voice was a caress over my skin, and my eyes fluttered open, taking him in.

How much did I have to drink tonight? Not enough that it would impact my judgment. Not enough to keep me from wanting this.

Him.

He'd been watching me all night.

Just like I'd been watching him.

I dropped my purse on the kitchen table, keys and all. I wondered if he could hear how fast my heart was beating from there with those demon senses of his. If it was any faster, I thought it would beat out of my chest.

From where I was standing, I could see out the large windows into the backyard, illuminated only by the light from the front entryway.

Even without looking at him, I could *feel* his presence behind me.

Damien's shadows wrapped around my arm, the tendril dancing over my skin in an intimate motion, like he was trailing a finger across my bare skin—

I closed my eyes, shuddering just from the small contact.

"Little witch..." He started, but before he could finish his thought, I turned around, bringing our bodies together.

He was so much taller than me, so bringing our mouths together was a challenge. Damien leaned down, taking my lips in his. And everything felt right again.

The kiss quickly turned deeper, more frantic. *Gods.* Kissing anybody else could never come close to my demon. He knew how to use his tongue, making me practically mewl against him. The way he could coax my mouth open for him, licking inside, those playful little bites against my lip...

And wasn't that the most unfair thing? He'd lived so much longer than me. Of course, he'd had his fair share of kissing other women. An idea that made me want to put a hex of my own on someone, because I didn't like the idea of anyone else touching him. Of his lips on anyone else.

But then his hands wrapped around my ass, lifting me up against his body, and it drained me of all rational thought.

My voice betrayed me, letting out a small moan when his erection brushed against my core as he pinned me against the wall. Taking me with his mouth again, he explored every inch—like he was trying to commit it to memory. Every swipe of his tongue against mine only spurred me on more.

My fingers brushed over his hardened length.

For *me.* This man—this demon—wanted *me.*

Maybe that was the thought that made me more brazen, bolder, but I didn't have it in me to care. I just wanted more. Needed it.

A low rumbling sound emitted from his throat when I moved my hand up, attempting to flick open the button on his pants.

I blinked. "Did you just... *growl* at me?"

"Little witch," he gritted out through his teeth. "I suggest you stop if you don't want to take this further."

I hummed in response, cupping him fully. "And what if I don't want to stop?" I ran a finger up his impressive bulge.

Fuck, I'd never wanted to have someone inside me so badly.

Damien leaned in close, enough for his lips to brush against my ear. For the rush of his warm breath to tickle my neck. "Then I'm going to take you to bed, Willow. And I'm not going to be able to hold back." He buried his nose in the crook of my neck. "Not when you smell this good."

He kissed the skin there, trailing a line up to my jaw with his lips, each touch like a brand against my skin.

I wanted it. Wanted him to mark me, for people to know I was *his*.

Wanted to not have to hide who this man was to me, because I was starting to wonder if I'd ever truly lived before he'd come into my life.

"I don't want you to hold back," I murmured, running my hands down the planes of his back as he sucked on my pulse point. "I want *you*," I moaned.

I couldn't keep it in any longer.

When he pulled away, his red eyes flared with need.

"*Fuck*." Any pretense of who he was gone—left behind in the bar, I assumed—and he looked down at me, perhaps more demon than man, but I *liked it*. "You want me to fuck you, Willow?"

"*Yes*," I agreed, and then I was back on my feet, spun around, his breath against my neck.

Damien stepped forward, pulling the zipper down slowly on my dress. If I was being honest, I'd only worn it for him—I liked to dress up, of course, but the way he'd looked at me when I walked downstairs... I'd never felt more beautiful, or desired.

I was finding I liked that with him. The way he could light up my body with just a kiss or a small touch.

He kissed my bare shoulder as he pushed the dress down my back, leaving me in my bra and the hip hugging lace panties I'd pulled on at the last minute. Damien's nimble fingers quickly made work of my bra clasp, and my nipples tightened as the cool air hit them.

Normally, I would have tried to hide myself, but how could I with the way he was looking at me? Like I was something to be treasured, worshiped.

"Fuck. You're perfect." He brought his hands up, cupping my breasts. When he ran his thumb over my nipple, I shuddered at how good it felt.

The lust was burning me alive. I'd never felt like this with anyone before—not this soul-encompassing need that I felt for him.

"Spread your legs for me," Damien murmured, bending down to capture my lips once more as his fingers dipped below the band of my panties—seeking, searching.

I was happy to comply. When was it last? *Months.* Maybe years.

"So wet, baby," he crooned, rubbing his fingers against my slit. "Did I do this to you?"

The only response I gave was a hum in agreement as he slipped a finger inside of me. He'd been driving me wild all night, teasing me with all of his lingering touches and heated glances.

I couldn't hold back my voice as he added another finger, exploring my folds. Trying to find that spot that he knew would drive me wild.

"Damien," I pleaded, my breaths growing heavy as I gave

into the growing pleasure. There was a part of me that was vaguely aware of how tightly I was grasping his shoulders, my legs growing unsteady underneath me.

I pulled away from him slightly, my eyes growing with awareness. He was still fully clothed, and we were standing in the hallway. Despite how eager I was, I didn't want our first time to be against the wall. Or on the floor.

"Bedroom," I panted, resting my forehead against his chest.

Is this my invitation? He thought, and I could almost feel the smirk on his face.

He could sleep in my bed for the rest of eternity if he kept up that movement with his fingers. I gasped. *Yes. Please.* I didn't want him on the couch anymore, anyway.

I could feel the loss as he pulled his fingers out of me, my juices coating them.

"I can't fucking wait to taste you," he murmured, putting them into his mouth, sucking my taste off of his digits as he maintained eye contact with me.

"*Oh.*" I squeaked out, as he gave one last lick of his lips.

"So sweet," he murmured, and then I was being lifted into his arms and carried towards my bedroom.

I was aching, squirming with need after he worked me up without letting me come.

Damien playfully swatted my ass. "Be still."

I'd never found getting spanked hot before, but the look in his eyes... *Damn.*

The demon's long legs quickly devoured up the space, and he kicked in the door before dropping me down on the bed.

His eyes were only slits as they traced over my naked body, from the line of my bare neck down to my tits and then to the panties that still covered me.

"What did I do to deserve you?" he mumbled, quickly stripping out of his clothes. Damien's eyes never left me as he dropped each article on the floor—until the only thing that remained was his briefs. The outline of his hardened length pressed against them, begging to be freed.

I sat up, reaching for his waistband, ready to give him the same treatment he had me. Sliding my thumbs into either side of his boxers, I pushed them down, eagerly freeing his cock.

Feeling him through his pants earlier had given me some idea of his size, but... My eyes widened. He was bigger than anyone I'd ever been with before, and I suddenly wondered what he would taste like. I ran a finger up his hardened length, watching him shudder at my touch.

Oh. I really liked that.

Only Damien clicked his tongue to the roof of his mouth, grabbing my hands before I could play with him any further. "Easy, witch. I have more plans for you."

I frowned. "But—"

Damien clicked his tongue, silencing me by pushing me down to the bed and threading his hand through my underwear. I expected him to roll them down, or slowly drag them off of my body, but instead, in a quick motion that left me dizzy, he ripped them off with a devilish grin.

"I liked those," I said with a frown.

He shook his head mischievously. "I'll get you new ones. Now, be a good girl and let me lick your pussy, Willow."

My cheeks flushed as he pulled me to the edge of the bed, positioning me so he could kneel in front of me. Placing his head level with my opening, he gripped the insides of my thighs, spreading them apart roughly.

Burying his head in between my legs, the first swipe of his tongue against my clit made me shudder. He groaned as his tongue lapped against me, like he couldn't get enough of my taste.

So sweet, his voice said into my mind.

"Damien," I begged, as he swirled and licked and drove me wild, not giving me the pressure that I needed. "I need—"

"Shhh, baby," he soothed, slipping his fingers back inside of me. Those apt fingers moved against my walls while he continued giving my clit attention with his mouth. "Gonna take care of you."

I didn't hold back my voice, the little noises he made me emit with each movement, or the moan when he sucked my clit into his mouth. There was no stopping the sensations unfurling inside of me, how close I was getting—

Damien looked up, his gaze connecting with mine even as he kneeled between my thighs. "Want you to come for me, Willow. Let me feel it on my tongue."

This time, his tongue darted inside of me, tasting me directly, and he brought his thumb to my clit, rubbing it in circles as his tongue explored my insides.

"Oh, *Gods.*"

He gave me a wicked grin. "No Gods here. Just your Demon."

My demon. I didn't care what anyone thought—he was. *Mine.*

That was the thought that I tipped over the edge with, with his tongue inside of me and those talented fingers making me come harder than I thought I ever had in my life.

Damien pulled back, his lips swollen, traces of me still glistening on them. I blushed. "Fuck, little witch. That was..." He placed a kiss on the inside of my thighs before standing up.

My heart was still racing. "Yeah." I didn't have the words, still panting from the exertion of my orgasm. No one had ever made me come so fast before, and I thought maybe it was all him. That the knowledge that he was the one playing with my body, lighting me on fire...

Sitting up, I looked between us, my finger reaching out to swipe the pre-cum from the head of his cock. I wanted him inside of me, wanted to know what it felt like to be joined together. He was so hard, his tip practically weeping, begging for a release of his own.

"Shit." I blurted out, a thought suddenly occurring to me. "I don't have any—" Protection.

When was the last time I'd needed it? I'd been too busy to date in forever, and even the thought of bringing home a man hadn't been in my mind in ages.

Damien looked pained, one hand wrapping around his length, squeezing slightly. "We don't have to do this."

"I'm on the pill," I murmured, reaching up to thread my fingers through his hair, wanting to be closer to him. "And I'm clean. So..." My eyes focused on his hand, how he was slowly working himself with it.

I'd never gone without condoms before—especially not with any humans I'd been with. But there was something about being with *him*—that it was us—that I didn't mind.

He groaned. "I don't want anything between us. Not the first time. Not when—" Giving a grunt of agreement, he dropped his forehead to my mine, kissing me roughly, our tongues tangling together. I could taste myself on his tongue.

"Please, Damien," I begged. "Need you."

Laying me down against the pillows, I wiggled my hips impatiently as he notched himself at my entrance, not giving me what I wanted. His entire body engulfed my frame, and I could barely take the time to revel in it, I was so eager.

"Patience, baby." He shook his head, the motion causing his hair to fall onto his forehead. "I don't want to hurt you."

I brushed some of the sweaty strands back with my fingers, reveling in the feel of his soft hair against my skin. "You won't,"

I promised. "You couldn't." Even in the short time I'd known him, I knew it to be true.

He closed his eyes, and when he opened them, the ring of red was almost entirely black. "You're sure?"

I nodded, wrapping my arms around his neck.

That was all it took before he pushed inside of me, slowly —inch by torturous inch.

"Fuck," he gritted out. "You're so tight."

"Only—" I moaned, "—because you're so *big*." *Fuck.* He'd basically stuffed me full, and he wasn't even fully inside of me yet.

More. Even with the fullness, I wanted more. My hips rocked against his involuntarily, pushing him in deeper. I could feel myself stretching around him, that feeling of fullness increasing as he worked his way inside of me.

"Look, how well you're taking me," he praised, as his eyes fixed on the spot where our bodies were connected. My body spread around him, greedily taking in his cock.

He stilled, letting me adjust to his size. As the slight pain faded away, a growing sense of pleasure replaced it.

"Willow." His voice was deep—raspy—in my ear. "I'm going to move now."

Damien kissed me before pulling out, almost all the way to the tip, before plunging back inside of me, burying himself to the hilt. I was so wet, his ministrations from earlier providing all the lubrication we needed.

Yes, Yes, Yes. I chanted, unsure if I was even forming verbal cohesive words at this point.

All I knew was it had never been like *this.*

Filthy. And yet I loved every moment of it.

The only sound in the room was our skin slapping against each other, my moans each time he hit *that* spot inside of me, and his small grunts as he focused on my body.

The delicious slide of his cock moving in and out of my body was too much, and yet...

"I need—" I said, vaguely aware that I didn't know what I needed, just that *more,* and I was losing my mind, but *more, more, more*—

He didn't stop, thrusting into me as his hands gripped the outside of my thighs tight enough I thought they might bruise. But then his shadows brushed against my skin, dancing across my nipples, almost like his tongue. When he did the same to my clit, my back arched off of the bed. The stimulation to every part of me was going to make me lose it.

Holy gods—"Don't stop," I moaned.

It was everything. It was too much. *"Damien,"* I moaned his name, loudly, thankful that we were alone in this house. That there was no fear of getting caught or being too loud.

Wrapping my legs around his hips, I intertwined them behind his back, forcing him in deeper.

My demon gave me another smirk—one that had no right being as sexy as it was—before bringing our mouths back together. His shadows were a caress around my entire body, only adding to how he was touching me.

"You feel so good inside of me," I encouraged, feeling him growing harder inside of me, knowing he must be close.

I wanted him to let go, to lose himself. Tightening my muscles, I clenched myself around him, squeezing his cock.

"Willow. Shit." He grimaced. *"Fuck.* I'm going to come if you don't stop that."

"Do it." I wasn't above begging for it. His cum—I licked my lips, rocking my hips in time with his movement. "Fill me up, Damien."

But—he shook his head, taking my lips in his, biting my lip slightly as he pulled away. "Need you to come again first."

His lips moved down to a nipple, sucking it into his mouth

as he massaged the other one, letting that tendril of darkness take over rubbing circles on my clit. It felt like his hands were *everywhere*, those shadows working as extensions of himself.

I'd already been close, but this time, I let go, burying my fingers into his shoulders, not even caring if I left marks from my fingernails as I came, crying out his name.

Damien kept up his thorough torture, switching his attention to my other nipple as he continued that glorious movement in and out of me.

My insides clenched around him, and he stilled, his mouth sliding off my breast with a wet *pop* as he gripped my hips, hardening even further inside of me.

"Fuck," he murmured, his eyes focused solely where we were joined together. Damien grit his teeth, burying himself to the hilt before letting go. I could feel the warmth spilling through my insides as he came, pouring inside of me on a shaky breath.

After he'd finished, he collapsed on top of me, holding me to his body before rolling both of us onto our sides as his cock softened inside of me.

"I didn't hurt you, right?" He asked, the concern evident in his voice. "I wasn't too rough?"

"No." I snuggled my head into his chest. "I liked it."

I'd never felt better. I was floating on air; the rightness surging through my body.

He kissed my forehead before shifting, like he was going to pull away.

I whined. "Don't. Not yet. I just wanna stay like this."

Tucking me back against his body, I wound my arms around his back, inhaling his spicy scent. Something about it calmed me—soothed me.

I wasn't going to evaluate why I liked it so much. Not yet.

"Willow," he whispered, and I realized my eyes had shut,

so warm and comforted by his presence that it had almost lulled me to sleep. "I'm going to get up now."

He pulled out, and I whimpered from the loss. I knew I needed to get up, to clean up, to take care of things, but I was boneless. Totally spent. I wasn't sure my legs had any strength left in them.

"Fuck, that's hot," he murmured, pushing his cum back inside of me.

Oh. Gods. That greedy little possessive side of me, the one that didn't want to imagine him with anyone else, liked that *very* much.

Damien came back to the bed a few moments later, and my eyes peeked open to find him holding a washcloth, wiping in between my thighs. He'd pulled on a pair of boxers, but left his chest bare.

After he seemed satisfied, he handed me a glass of water, getting me to drink it before slipping back under the covers.

Damien's arms wrapped around me, and I snuggled into his chest, letting my eyes close as I drifted off to sleep.

Some part of me recognized I shouldn't trust him, shouldn't let him into my heart—but I wasn't sure I cared anymore. Not when he was so gentle with me, especially when it mattered. When he'd shown, over and over, how he was here for me.

And if I wasn't careful—I was going to fall for him completely.

I kissed her forehead, watching her sleep.

She looked so peaceful, so... calm like this. With the morning light bathing her face in gold, a serene smile spread across her face. She was an angel, a goddess. A gift I didn't deserve.

I'd never known how good it would feel—to wake up like this. To spend a night in each other's arms. I was no stranger to sex, but last night... It felt like a first for me.

Brushing a hair out of her face, I held my breath as she stirred slightly.

"Hi," she murmured, voice rough from sleep.

"Good morning." I kissed her cheek, because even if I was trying to be good, it was hard to keep my hands off of her.

"What's the plan for today?" I asked, curling an arm around my witch.

Willow stretched her arms, the sheet moving back from the motion, exposing her cute pink tits. My mouth watered.

"Mmm." Her groggy voice groaned. "I'm hungry. Should we have breakfast?" Her body cuddled closer to me, pressing her nipples against my chest.

I held in the groan I felt from the feeling, trying to focus on the woman in front of me. On her priorities—instead of how I was already half hard, just from the feel of her body against mine. "What about the bakery? Do we need to go help Luna?"

She waved me off. "No, she's got it. She told me to take the day off." Willow sat up, wincing slightly as she moved. "Maybe she knew I'd be sore."

A devilish grin spread over my face. "I think I know just the thing that will help."

I wanted to make her feel better, since I was the reason for it. She'd taken all of me so well, and I couldn't help how much of a satisfied male that made me.

Ripping the sheets off our bodies, I picked her up in my arms. Her still naked form made my current plan much easier. Willow's soft curves pressed against my body, and I couldn't help but appreciate her figure. How lucky I was that she'd picked me. Setting her on the bathroom counter, I got everything ready for her.

Moving to her giant claw-foot tub, I started the water running, adding some soothing oils and sea salt to help her muscles relax. As it filled, I went and grabbed a few candles, leaving them on various surfaces in the room. It created a beautiful ambiance, illuminating both of us in candlelight when I flicked the light off.

"Wow," she said sleepily. "Such service."

"Have to take care of my little witch," I said, kissing her forehead as I held out a hand, helping her into the tub.

"Ohhh," she moaned as she slid into the warm water, closing her eyes and tipping her head back against the rim. "If you're going to spoil me like this, I won't be able to let you go."

"Willow—" I hated that she thought this thing between us was temporary. That there was any doubt in her mind about what I was feeling. But I couldn't tell her that. It was too soon.

"Not now," my witch whispered. "Please."

Stripping off my boxers, I slowly slid into the water behind her, wrapping my arms around her waist. I couldn't stop touching her. I needed to, if only to calm that instinct inside of me. The one that screamed *Mine*. I wanted to claim her, to mark her, for the world to know exactly who she belonged to.

Later. It wasn't time for that yet. There was still so much she didn't know.

"Better?" I asked, massaging her thighs.

Willow hummed in agreement, leaning her head back to rest against my shoulder. She shut her eyes, looking totally at ease.

After I'd washed her hair, we stayed in the bath until the water ran cold, neither one of us wanting to break this perfect bubble.

She was right. We could talk about everything later. I just wanted to enjoy my time with her for now.

Her eyes widened as she entered the kitchen. "You weren't kidding when you said you know how to make breakfast."

I'd fried eggs, cooked some bacon, and even made pumpkin pancakes after leaving Willow to get ready, knowing we'd never leave her bedroom if I stayed in there.

My eyes trailed over her body in an obvious perusal. She'd pulled on a cozy white sweater and a tan overall dress, tying her hair up into a ponytail with an orange and white polka dot scrunchie.

"Hi," I said, giving her a small smile before she slid in behind me, wrapping her arms around my torso.

"Hi," she responded to my back. "I like you in my kitchen," she murmured.

"Oh?" I felt smug. *Me too.* Mainly because I liked being here too. It was crazy how quickly I'd become comfortable in this house. How little I wanted to leave. But I owed all of that to the witch hugging me from behind.

I'd be here as long as she wanted me to. A month wouldn't be enough time with her. I knew it now. Especially after last night. The bond I'd felt strengthening between us with each movement...

Rubbing my hand over my heart, I gave a deep, contented sigh. I'd never felt more peaceful than I did here, with her in my arms.

"Hmm?" Willow asked, but I just shook my head.

"Shall we eat?"

She grinned, grabbing my hand and leading me over to the table. "Gods yes."

Willow sat down at one end of the table, guiding me into the seat directly next to her. Part of me liked that I was close enough to press my knee into hers, that I didn't have to lose contact for even a moment. It made my body purr, the prolonged connection between us.

Willow quickly devoured the pumpkin pancakes, barely taking a break between bites. I finished my plate fast as well, having worked up quite an appetite from last night's events. If we were going to keep *that* up, I needed to feed her properly.

"*Ohmygods,*" she moaned, her mouth full of pancake. "This is so good. *Whatthehell.*" She swallowed, taking a deep drink of milk before speaking again. "Where did you learn to do this?"

I shrugged. "When you've lived as long as me, it's hard not to get bored." I propped my chin on my hands, watching her dig in. "Every decade, I picked up a new hobby to keep things interesting. I learned to play the piano. Dance. How to paint—

though I'm not very good at that." He wrinkled up his nose. "I just ended up with more paint on *me* than on the canvas."

She giggled. "I'd love to have seen that."

"Most things from the human world make their way over to ours. Your culture. The demons who are working here bring it back, and, well..." Running my hands through my hair, I stared down at my empty plate. "Cooking was enjoyable. I was good at it. Never quite got the hang of baking, though."

Willow's mouth was hanging open before she recovered. "That's okay. You don't like sweets anyway, right?"

Leaning over, I took her mouth into mine, slipping my tongue inside. She tasted like pancakes and syrup and *Willow*. I practically groaned at the way she exploded onto my taste buds.

She blinked as I pulled away, her eyes glazed over in a haze. "What was that for?"

I licked my lip before running my thumb over the corner of her mouth. "So sweet." I smirked. "Maybe I do like it, after all."

Her cheeks flushed as she took another bite.

Part of me knew I should get up and start cleaning, but I just kept watching my witch eat instead. Satisfied, I let my chest rumble as she shoveled another bite into her mouth.

"What should we do today? I've been wondering what else you have left on your *fall must-dos* list. How much education do I have left?"

Willow stared up at me, and I rubbed my chest again.

Fuck. Was it that loud? I couldn't control it. Part of my shape-shifting abilities was being able to change forms at will, but the instincts came with the territory. The purring came whenever I felt especially content or fulfilled. I'd hardly ever experienced that level of satisfaction before this, though. Before Willow.

"Well, what do you think?"

She blinked. "Sorry, about what?"

"About our plans for the day. I was thinking we still had those pumpkins..." I grinned, pointing at the two perfect pumpkins waiting to be carved. They'd been sitting on the counter staring at me over the last few days, and I felt taunted.

Sure, I'd experienced a lot of things from human culture, but we didn't carve pumpkins in the demon realm. And if it meant more time with Willow, I'd gladly take it.

Even if I was ignoring Zain's *summons*. My mission seemed less important now, knowing who exactly sat at my side. My brother could wait a little longer.

"Oh." Willow's green eyes lit up with excitement. "*Yes!*" She clapped her hands. "We definitely need to do that. I have to go dig out the box with the tools from the attic."

"I'll come with you," I said instantly

"No, it's okay." She shook her head, wincing. "It's pretty messy up there. All of my parent's stuff, well... I'll get it." She kissed the side of my head as she rose from her chair.

"Okay." I sighed, wanting to help her but not wanting to push too hard. "I'll clean up from breakfast."

"Perfect." Willow gave me a smile, setting her dishes in the sink before promptly disappearing.

There was nothing that could ruin my mood today. Not with Willow by my side.

There were pumpkin guts everywhere.

On every conceivable surface.

In Willow's hair.

"What did you do?" I asked, wiping a drip off of her cheek. "Blow the damn thing up?"

143

She giggled. "Luna likes to use the seeds and the insides for the bakery. I might have... overestimated my magic." There was a sheepish grin on her face, and I couldn't help cupping her cheeks with my hands.

I enjoyed how they engulfed her face, much like my hands did with her tits. They were the perfect size, considering I could practically cup them in my hands.

"Do you need me to clean you up again, little witch?"

She gave me a wicked smile. "Are you going to dirty me up first?"

Swallowing roughly, I willed myself not to think those thoughts. We were supposed to be carving pumpkins, not christening the kitchen table.

"Later," I agreed, picking up the tool. "First, we're going to carve these things."

"Right." Willow nodded, moving to stand behind me. "So... what are you doing?"

I shook my head. "It's a surprise."

Carving pumpkins was much harder than it looked, and I was pretty sure mine looked like absolute shit, but at least I'd done it. I was grateful for the opportunity to try new activities here, things that I never had the chance to do in the demon realm.

We certainly didn't have pumpkins lying around in wait for being carved.

"Ta-da!" Willow turned around her pumpkin, showing me the opposite side. "It's you!" She'd carved a cat out, complete with a tail and glowing eyes.

I laughed. "That's... amazing."

"What'd you do?" She asked, coming around to see mine.

Sheepishly, I stepped away, revealing my design. "I know it's not very good, but..."

"A tree?" She made a face. "Why?"

"It's... supposed to be a willow tree." I winced.

"Oh." Our eyes connected, and I could detect a faint blush on her cheekbones. "That's... *Damien*." She clasped her hands over her heart. "No one's ever done anything like that for me before."

I pulled her into my arms, placing a kiss on the top of her head. How did I tell her I felt the same way? No one had ever cared for me before like she did. No one had made me feel like she did.

It was crazy, since we'd known each other for two weeks, but I already felt closer to her than I did to anyone else in my life. My brother was the only person who came close, but we weren't really *friends*. Sometimes it just felt like a business relationship between us.

"You deserve it," I said instead. "Besides, you did the same for me."

Her cheeks deepened in color. "Yeah. I guess I did."

Leaning down, I took her lips in mine, a gentle peck to convey my gratitude, but it slowly deepened into more. Running my fingers through her hair, I reveled in the way the silky strands slipped through them.

"Damien," she mumbled against my lips. "I want—"

"I know," I agreed, lifting her up by the hips, reveling in the feeling of her as she wrapped her legs around my back, holding on.

I carried her to the bedroom, my ever hardening erection pressed against her center.

And then I stripped her down, and we got lost in each other.

In these feelings I couldn't quite acknowledge.

We were both insatiable, like last night had only lit a fire in us we couldn't quell. Once wouldn't be enough.

It would never be enough.

"I need more time." I hated bringing myself this low, begging him for this, but I had no other choice. I needed more time with Willow. I couldn't let her go yet.

And that was why I was here, on my knees, bringing myself to a position I'd sworn never to be for my brother.

Zain crossed his arms over his chest, raising an eyebrow. "Why? What exactly are you afraid of, little brother?"

I grit my teeth. "You know exactly what I'm afraid of."

"I need her." He sighed. "You can't keep me away forever."

"Just... give me until Halloween, at least. Please. Willow needs her sister."

"Very well." My brother waved his hand, dismissing me. "You have until then."

I closed my eyes, letting the shadows take me home.

To Willow.

The only place I wanted to be.

There was something about knowing I had someone at home waiting for me that made me giddier to leave the shop each day than I ever had before. Maybe that was what made the time pass quicker than it felt like it ever had before.

Damien.

I smiled to myself as I wiped down the counter, eyes focused on the clock, waiting for Eryne to come in for her shift. I'd been cleaning for the last hour, and as soon as she took over, I'd be free.

To head home to my demon, and whatever festive activity we'd choose for tonight. In the last week, we'd watched countless Halloween movies—I had to educate him, after all—as well as tried all my favorite kinds of candy. I was determined to find something he liked. I wasn't below resorting to black licorice, if that was what it took.

I especially liked it when he'd give up halfway through and pin me to the couch, kissing me roughly with that mouth I'd grown so fond of. Sometimes it felt like he was trying to commit every inch of me to memory, like if he kissed me enough, I would never fade from his thoughts.

Thinking about him leaving—my house, my bed, my life—hurt, so I tried not to. To just appreciate this thing between us, no matter how short-lived it would be.

We hadn't talked about our feelings, though. Every time he brought it up, I brushed him off. Everything was so good, and I didn't want to ruin it by talking about the future.

I had to remind myself that no matter how he made me feel —when he was so tender and caring with me—that this wasn't a relationship.

But October was coming to a close faster than I'd have liked.

So was the month he'd promised me. The town's big Halloween party was only a few days away.

Our pumpkins we'd carved were now sitting on my front porch, complete with flickering lights I enchanted to never burn out. Sure, I could have used electric LED candles, but where was the fun in that?

Some nights, we would sit on the porch swing outside as the sun set, hardly speaking a word. It was almost like we didn't need to.

And losing ourselves in each other's bodies every night... I was pretty sure Damien had turned me into some sort of sex demon, because I couldn't get enough of him. He'd leave me exhausted, totally boneless, and I would fall asleep as soon as my head hit the pillow.

I grinned, just thinking about whatever he had planned for me tonight. Even as I taught him human things, I was learning new things about myself too—my preferences. How he could key up my body and turn me on with just the faintest of touches. The whisper of a touch, the brush of his powers against me, or the feeling of his sharp canines brushing against my throat.

I shivered at the thought.

"You look smitten," Luna murmured as I spun into the kitchen.

"What?" I came to a stop, attempting not to drop my armful of dishes that I'd brought with me, using my free time to tidy up the front of the bakery. Were my cheeks pink? "N-no." How vehemently could I deny it?

Especially when it was true.

Okay, I *was* smitten. Too smitten. It was a problem. "I... I like him, okay?" I dropped my shoulders in defeat as I dumped the dirty pitchers and spoons into the sink. "It's never been like this for me before."

"And he feels the same way?" Luna asked. I could tell she was skeptical of Damien—and maybe that was fair. It wasn't like I'd really told her what was happening between us. Who he was.

"I mean, I haven't asked him for sure, but I think so." It felt like he did.

"What are you afraid of?" She probed, and I folded, just like always.

I didn't want to say it, but I couldn't stop the words that slipped from my lips. My deepest fears, brought to life. "That he'll leave. Decide I'm not worth it and walk away."

"Willow." Luna's voice was soft. Reassuring. And yet filled with so much care and compassion, my heart nearly broke at the love pouring out of her. "You don't even know how amazing you are, do you?"

"You *have* to say that." I shook my head. "You're my little sister."

"No." She shook her head. "I mean it. You always take care of everyone but yourself. Even me. It's time to put yourself

149

first. Besides, if that man really leaves, he's not who I thought he was, anyway."

"He's a demon," I murmured, turning around and facing the sink.

"What?"

"Nothing." Turning on the sink, I let the dishes fill up with water before washing them.

When I finally turned back around, Luna rolled her eyes at me. "I'm just saying. I've seen the way he looks at you."

"Like what?" I was almost too afraid to say it.

"Like you're his entire world."

"Oh."

"Yeah. *Oh.*" She pinched my arm. "If you don't tell that man how you feel about him, I'll do it myself."

"*Luna,*" I complained, drawing out her name. "It's still new. I don't want to ruin it."

She raised an eyebrow, and I held up my arms. "Fine, fine! I'm going home now."

Luna raised her fingers, giving me a little wave. "Tell your man I say hello."

I rolled my eyes as I grabbed my stuff, heaving my bag over my shoulder. "Don't stay too long yourself," I added. "Goddess knows you could use some time away from this place. You practically live here, I swear."

She didn't dignify *that* with a response.

Waving goodbye to Eryne at the counter on my way out, I headed home.

To the demon waiting for me.

"Damien!" I shouted, tossing my keys on the front table and my tote bag onto my designated stuff chair. "I'm home!"

Part of me liked being able to say that to someone. Sure, I used to say it to my sister—and to my cat—but now, knowing that the being in this house was mine, even if it was just for now, made me giddy.

"I brought home some of the extra scones Luna made today," I added, carrying the box into the kitchen. "They're pumpkin and chocolate chip." I was watering just thinking about the contents. As if I hadn't had two this morning.

"What are we doing tonight?" His arms wrapped around my shoulders as he placed a kiss on my temple. "Does this town have any other fun festivities I should know about?"

"Have you ever gone bobbing for apples before?"

Damien looked horrified. "Willow. What?"

I laughed, unable to keep a straight face. "I'm kidding. Though you wouldn't believe what some of the kids here can do. They're champs." I brushed a hair back from my face, grabbing the other bag of supplies I'd brought home with me. "I thought maybe we could make caramel apples and then just watch a movie. There's a new one on tonight."

Slowly, I was going to convert him to like my silly Halloween romance movies. I had no idea what he watched before meeting me, but I'd watch them all year long if people let me. We'd already watched Halloweentown and Hocus Pocus, two of my favorites, but I had an entire cabinet full of options.

"Mmm. Sounds good. But I have an idea before that."

"You do?"

He nodded, taking my hand and guiding me outside to the back patio.

"Is this..." I looked back at him. "Did you do all of this?"

Damien gave me another nod. Not only had he strung a

canopy of lights over the backyard, but he'd laid out a blanket —laid out with a complete picnic and a glass of wine. The last rays of sunset showed through the trees, lighting up their orange and yellow leaves. I loved New England in the fall. Truly, even though I could have moved anywhere, I couldn't imagine being anywhere but here.

"It's probably not as good as the one at the festival, but..." He pulled the lid off of a dish, exposing a freshly made pumpkin pie.

"Damien..." My eyes watered. "You made me my favorite pie?"

"Of course." He kissed my forehead as we both settled onto the blanket. "Anything for my little witch."

"You gotta stop spoiling me," I murmured, staring up at his chiseled jaw as I settled against him. "Or I'm never going to let you go."

My admission was too close to the truth, and I promptly shut my mouth. I didn't want to ruin this moment with that conversation. It could wait.

He gave me a lopsided grin before starting to unveil the rest of the dishes. It must have taken him all day to do this. Damien placed a glass of wine in my hands, and I took a sip, enjoying the flavors as they blossomed on my tongue.

The lighting, the ambiance, it was all simply perfect. He was perfect. How could he be anything but? He'd come into my life in the most unexpected of ways, but he fit so perfectly.

Fit with *me* so perfectly.

I gave a happy sigh, leaning my head against his shoulder. The aroma of the food wafted towards my nose, and I was suddenly starving. I couldn't wait to try everything he'd made for us.

"Oh. And one more thing." He pressed a button, and a low, soothing melody started playing. "Now it really is perfect."

I shook my head in disbelief. He'd really thought of everything, hadn't he?

Which led me to the question I'd been asking myself for the last week...

How was I going to let him go?

"I'm so full," I bemoaned, talking to the black cat who laid at my feet.

I didn't know why he still insisted on sleeping in cat form some nights, but part of me didn't want to complain, either. As much as I preferred falling asleep wrapped in his arms, I enjoyed having his little bundle of weight at my feet.

His little vampire teeth were visible as he laid on his back, all sprawled out in cat form on my bed. One paw was dangling over the edge. Damien in cat form was simply adorable.

Moving my hand to scratch his head, he nuzzled against my palm. I stifled a giggle. "You're pretty cute like this, you know?"

Damien shifted in a flash, lying on his arm on top of my comforter, his fangs still poking out over his bottom lip. "And what about now, little witch?"

Much like that first night where I'd kicked him off the bed, he'd shifted completely naked. I was wearing my favorite nightgown, which wasn't particularly sexy. And with him draped on top of my bed like *that*...

"Damien!" I flushed red, throwing my arm over my face. "You can't just—"

Nuzzling his face into my neck, he ran his sharp canines over the sensitive skin of my throat. "Can't what?"

I wondered what it would feel like if he were to bite me. He didn't need to drink blood, as far as I was aware. At least, I'd never seen him do it—but did those sharp teeth serve another purpose? Every time they touched my skin, they sent sensations straight to my clit. Like I could explode with one touch.

"Do *that*." Not looking, I gestured at his body.

Not that I needed to look at him to know what his body looked like. I'd memorized every line, traced every one of his abs with my tongue. I'd gotten more comfortable with him than I had with any human who I'd ever slept with in the past.

They all paled compared to Damien, anyway. My passionate, caring, thorough lover, who knew exactly how to use his tongue and fingers.

And don't get me started on when he used his magic on me.

In a flash, he'd moved, pinning me to the bed, his muscular arms positioned over me. "What about now?"

"*Please*," I moaned, not sure what I was begging for. Him to stop, or him to keep going?

He kissed at my throat, his talented tongue making me squirm within a matter of minutes.

More. I needed him brushing his shadows over my nipples and my clit.

I wondered to what extent he could use his powers—how *else* he might use those tendrils of darkness on me. Inside of me—

Damien's nostrils flared, like he could smell my growing arousal. Sense how wet I was getting, just from his teeth and my lewd thoughts. "What are you thinking about, little witch?"

"Nothing." I blushed, shaking my head.

He raised an eyebrow. "Willow." He pressed his hips into mine, and I let out a small moan. "Tell me, baby."

I shook my head as he started working my nightgown up my hips, exposing my purple underwear covered in ghosts.

He rocked into me, pressing up against that thin fabric, as his lips connected with the pulse point on my neck. Damien's fangs dragged over the sensitive skin—not enough to pierce it, but to send shudders of pleasure through me. "Tell me," he murmured, "and I'll give you what you want."

"I-I was thinking about how else you could use your shadows." I knew my cheeks were as pink as ever. "Besides just... *you know.*"

He chuckled roughly, nibbling on my ear. "Do you want me to fill you up, baby? Stuff you so full of me you can barely breathe?"

"*Yes,*" I choked out. "I want that."

Who was this girl, and what had she done with Willow? I'd never had the courage to ask for what I wanted before. Even if I was still embarrassed. Even if he had to encourage the words.

It was like I'd come to life completely from just his one touch.

And I wanted more, and more, and more.

The question was... would I ever stop wanting him?

damien

This girl. My little witch.

"Willow," I rasped out, already out of my mind just from her suggestion. I'd never done *that*, not with anyone. But what she was asking me... "Are you sure?"

Her eyelids fluttered hazily as I pressed myself against her again.

"Mhm. Please, Damien. I need you inside of me."

Pulling her cute little nightdress off her body, I took my time to kiss down her collarbone and stomach before coming to her hips.

Purple ghosts. "Fuck me, these are so adorable." Her collection of Halloween undergarments never failed to make me smile. I kissed one of her hip bones, and then the other. "You drive me crazy, Willow."

She hummed in response as I slowly peeled her panties off, nipping her inner thighs as I went.

"Come here," I said, laying down and patting my chest. "I want you to sit on my face."

Willow scrambled to sit on my chest, her thighs parted around me.

"Are you sure?" She looked concerned, like she didn't know that I would die without this. That I'd been thirsty for her taste only.

"Mhm. Let me taste that sweet pussy, baby. I want you to come all over my mouth."

"O-kay," she said, and I helped guide her up to my mouth, my hands on the outside of her thighs as she settled her cunt over my lips.

With the first slide of my tongue against her wet folds, her hands darted out to hold on to the headboard.

"Oh," she cried. Her legs were squeezing against my head, my nose pressed against her clit as she rode my face, and with each flick of my tongue inside of her, she moved in earnest, rocking her hips as I licked up every drop of her.

I kept up my pace, those slow languid licks, even as her hips moved faster, and I could feel how close she was getting, the tiny tremors of pleasure that ran through her.

There was nothing I wanted more than to feel her orgasm on my tongue, so I didn't stop. Even as she cried my name. As her thighs tightened their grip.

Let go, I coaxed her. *Come for me, little witch.* I added my thumb to her clit, rubbing it in circles as I kept fucking her with my tongue.

My girl didn't hold back. And when she came, body shuddering, her insides squeezing around my tongue, it was better than anything I'd ever imagined.

And so was the realization that I didn't want to do this with anyone else. Never again. Because Willow was mine. Her intoxicating coffee and vanilla scent had crept into my veins, and I couldn't get her out. Didn't want to get her out.

I wanted to feast on her taste for the rest of my life. One human lifetime wasn't enough. I needed more.

This may have started because of the bond I sensed between

us, but I knew the truth now. I'd felt it creeping up on me over the last week, but there was no doubt in my mind as she let go for me.

I was an idiot to think anything else could have been the cause.

Guiding her body off of my face after the aftershocks of her orgasm had subsided, I gave her a smirk. "You taste so damn good, baby."

Her cheeks were pink—maybe from her orgasm—but I liked how my words affected her.

Willow leaned down to kiss me, not hesitating, even knowing that she'd taste herself on my lips.

Fuck, but that was hot.

She perched herself on my torso, each one of her strong thighs positioned against my legs, and I could feel her wetness pooling there as her tongue battled mine.

It made me even more eager to bury myself in her. Feeling how ready she was. How eager she was to take my cock.

"Fuck," I muttered as she pulled away, biting my lower lip as she disconnected our lips. I was painfully hard—something she'd be aware of soon, if she couldn't already feel my hardness pressed against her ass. "Need you," I panted. My hands went to her hips, loving the way her body felt in my hands.

Would I ever be able to get over it? How perfectly we fit together? How each one of her curves felt like they were made for my hands?

She rocked backwards, rubbing her cute little ass against my cock, and I let out a deep moan.

"Willow—" I warned, but clearly, I hadn't needed to at all.

Because she picked her hips up, even as I kept my hands on her waist, and positioned herself over me. Ready to spear herself on my cock.

And when Willow guided me inside of her, it was all I could

do to squeeze my eyes shut, trying not to blow my load too soon. Being inside of her—*fuck*, nothing compared.

She splayed her hand over her stomach. "Gods. I can feel you *everywhere.*"

"Feels like you were made for me, little witch." The truth came spilling out from my lips. It was true—even if I hadn't meant to say it yet. But the pieces fit. We... fit.

I let Willow set the pace, moving back and forth on my cock, feeling the way her body jolted each time her clit hit the base of my shaft.

"Damien, I—I can't," she cried. "I'm going to come."

Yes. Yes. Give me everything, I agreed, watching her tits bounce as she lost herself in the sensations.

"Tell me you're mine," I commanded, needing to hear the words. Needing to know that what I felt was true—real.

"I'm yours," she agreed, rolling her hips as she rode me. "All yours. Only yours."

"Mine," I repeated, grabbing her neck to bring it down to me so I could fuse our mouths together. My hips thrust up to meet hers, and I could feel the way she was clenching down around me. So close.

Fuck, I loved kissing her. I didn't think I'd ever tire of taking her mouth. She tasted sweet, and I could still detect a hint of the pumpkin pie she'd eaten earlier.

I fucking loved her addiction to pumpkin.

Maybe I just plain loved *her.*

But it was too soon to tell her that. This was too new. And I certainly wasn't some fool of a human who would blurt it out during sex.

"Damien," she cried. "I need—"

That was what unleashed the beast inside of me, and I couldn't hold back any longer. I used my hold on her waist to help her move—up and down, up and down, each slide of her against my cock, providing me with another moan.

My shadows curled possessively around her body, pressing up against practically every erogenous zone. Her throat, a light squeeze. Her nipples, that sucking sensation I knew drove her crazy. And one pressed against her back hole, nothing more than a finger's press, but she cried out. I used my powers like hands, cupping her breasts, squeezing them, even as I helped her ride me, watching her bounce on my cock. Her breasts moved with the motion, and I was in awe as I watched her.

Willow's head fell back as her eyes shut. *It's too much,* she sobbed into my mind.

You can take it, I soothed, my hips moving in time with hers as we worked together. Giving her everything she'd asked for —everything she needed. *Eyes open,* I added, nuzzling my forehead against hers. "Want to watch you come," I murmured.

She came without warning, a squeeze around my cock, like she wanted to milk me dry. I was so deep—basically pressed up against her womb, and somehow, the idea of that made me tip over the edge.

Of painting her insides with my cum. Filling her up.

She'd asked me to that first night, and, like a fool, I couldn't resist. Something about knowing she would fall asleep with my cum dripping out of her made me feral. Weak. Uncontrollable.

I could feel the telltale signs of my own release—my balls tightened, and I held Willow in place, with me buried to the hilt inside of her—as I spilled every last drop.

And even when we'd collapsed on the bed—boneless and spent—I didn't pull out of her.

"Mmm," Willow murmured sleepily, curling against me. "I think you've ruined me for anyone else, Damien."

That was the idea, baby, I thought, but I didn't say it out loud.

I just wrapped my arms around her and fell into a deep sleep.

I woke up with sweat dripping down my back, pulse racing. Willow laid next to me, the sheets tugged up her body as she dozed peacefully.

Ripping the sheets from my body, I launched myself out of the bed, silently slipping out of the room. Something was suffocating me, and all I knew was I needed to get out of there, needed air, needed space, needed—

In the kitchen, I guzzled down a glass of water.

Why was it bothering me so much? But I knew why. Even if it wasn't real.

Closing my eyes, all I could see was *red*. Blood. They'd...

"Are you okay?" Willow wrapped her arms around my bare torso. "I heard you get up." She'd pulled a robe on, the soft fabric brushing against my skin in a warm embrace.

No. No, I wasn't okay. When I turned to her, I knew my face looked pained.

"Just a bad dream," I murmured, burying my face in her hair. Inhaling her scent.

Reminding myself that she was here.

And nothing was going to happen to her. I'd make sure of that.

"What happened?" Her voice was quiet as she rubbed the muscles in my back—soothing, like she could get rid of all my tension just from her touch. My magical fucking girl.

I shook my head against her hair. "I don't want to talk about it."

"Damien..." Her hands moved down to my lower back. "You can talk to me, you know. I'm here for you."

I heaved out a sigh. "It's not..."

How would she understand? I couldn't even figure out my own irrational fears and worries, and trying to explain them to her? Impossible.

Especially when there was so much I was still keeping from her. But I'd tell her soon. All of it. The truth about us.

Right now, I just wanted to hold her. To remind myself that she was here. That *this* was real. No matter what would come in the future, I had this.

When I made eye contact with her, she looked up at me with such bright eyes. So hopeful. So curious.

Why wasn't I letting her in?

"I'm scared," I said, my voice so low it was essentially a whisper.

"Of what?" Her arms tightened around my back as she hugged my chest.

Losing you. I couldn't say it out loud, so I said it into her mind instead.

"Oh." Willow's sweet voice slipped out.

Not wanting to go another minute without holding her, I wrapped my arms around her thighs, lifting her up so I could carry her back into the bedroom, just like that. Willow wrapped her legs around me, clinging on like a baby bear.

She didn't unwrap her arms from around my back even as I sat on the bed.

"Little witch," I murmured, running my hands through the silky strands of her hair. "You have to let go now."

"Uh-uh." Her lips curled up into a smile. "You're always

taking care of me. Let me take care of you for once. Till your dream goes away."

I didn't think it ever would, but I wouldn't tell her that.

"Okay." I wouldn't argue with her when I loved the way she snuggled against me.

Like she was *mine*.

After we'd gotten comfortable on the bed, Willow curled up next to my body once again.

Laying her head on my shoulder, she traced circles over my bare chest. "Why don't you tell me about your family?"

"Hm?"

Of everything she could have asked... Did she even know how close that hit to home?

"You never talk about them," she said sadly. "Or your mom. Not really. I want to know everything about you, Damien."

I'd opened my mouth to tell her that wasn't true, that I talked about them, but I couldn't deny it. And knowing what was between us, what I felt for her... I didn't want to hold it in anymore.

So I started talking. I told her about my mom, and how she'd been my favorite person in the entire world. How when she'd died, leaving me alone with my father and half-brother, there had been a vacancy that could never quite be filled. A hole in my heart.

One she'd filled.

How I wished my mom could have met Willow. Seen what an amazing woman she was.

I left out the blood.

I could still feel it against my fingers. Hear my voice screaming out for help. But the memory of my mother's death was being overwritten with my dream about Willow's.

And even so... I didn't stop. I told her about growing up in

163

the demon realm. Training to fight in my father's battles. Serving as his right-hand man. King of the Demons.

And, later, being relegated to an over-glorified errands boy. Serving my brother, the Crown Prince. Who'd take over for our father one day, after he found his bride.

Long after she'd fallen asleep, I still kept holding her, stroking her hair, mystified that out of every person in this world, she was the one chosen for me.

I love you, I thought to myself alone, cradling her body into mine.

I tugged at the collar of my costume for the town's Halloween party. The damn thing itched my neck, and I still couldn't figure out how I'd let Willow convince me to dress up like this.

The truth was, all it took was one flash of those green eyes, and I'd cave every time.

So she'd dressed us up—in Victorian-style costumes, as a Vampire and a Witch.

"You can put those pointy teeth to use," my witch teased me, her thumb running over a sharp canine.

"I think you just want to find out what it feels like when I bite you," I teased her back.

Her cheeks pinked. "Maybe."

I purred in response. I wanted to claim her. To see my mark on her neck.

Everything felt so right. I knew I could no longer keep denying the truth. How much I loved her. Why we fit together so perfectly. Why everything with her was *more.*

But it also terrified me to admit it. To say the words. What if she didn't want *that?* Every time I'd tried to bring up what we were, she'd brushed me off. Had she only ever been looking for this? Something casual?

My deadline was looming. I'd asked my brother for an extra month. Not even being the son of the Demon King could deny what was next.

The fates had foretold that the next demon king would marry a great witch. I was sent here to do just that. To find Zain's consort—*his* fated mate—not a woman to call my own. Perks of being the illegitimate son of the current Demon King, I supposed. I was forced to serve Zain's bidding. Like finding him a wife in this accursed place was anything short of easy. But of all the demons, I had the easiest time blending in. Being unnoticed.

Passing as human. Four months had passed since my brother had sent me to the human realm searching for *his bride*.

Despite my little roadblock—I'd found her, to my worst horror.

Because the witch who was fated to sit by my brother's side... was none other than Willow's sister. *Luna.*

Time was running out.

The worst part was I knew Willow didn't belong with me, anyway. She was too bright and beautiful to go back to my world of darkness. This place—this town of witches—it was where she belonged. I could feel it. Though that didn't stop me from wanting her.

I couldn't believe that she'd been here for twenty-eight years and I hadn't known that she was here. That she existed at all. But... in all my years of life, I'd hardly come to the human realm. I'd never expected to find my mate here.

"There's my handsome demon," my girl beamed, coming to stand by my side and sliding her arm around my waist.

"Hi, Wil," I murmured before dropping a kiss on the top of her head.

"Hi." Her eyes lit up. She'd curled her hair, letting it fall down around her in waves, and an old-fashioned witch hat sat on top. My witch looked perfect, down to the little star earrings and her striped stockings.

I was obsessed. I couldn't wait to take them off of her later.

"You look beautiful. I love this." I fiddled with the cape that was tied around her neck.

She giggled. "It's not too much?"

I groaned. "That would be impossible. Nothing you do could ever be too much."

"Oh." Her cheeks pinked.

How did I get her to understand I meant every word? I brushed a hair away from her face before playing with her earring. "You look stunning. It's so you. I can't imagine you being anything less than that." I dragged a finger down her throat. "I almost don't want anyone else to see you like this."

She kissed my cheek. "You're the sweetest demon I've ever met."

"I'm the *only* demon you've ever met," I grunted.

"That you know of."

"And we're going to keep it that way," I growled, pinning her in my arms as she laughed.

Kissing her, because if this was all the time we had left, I wanted to savor every bit of it.

Especially if it was all we'd have left.

All Hallows' Eve. My favorite night of the year was here.

The air was filled with children laughing, candy wrappers tearing, and the smell of sugar in the air. Damien was at my side, his hand curled around mine, hardly an inch left between us.

It was the perfect Halloween night, the moon high in the sky, shining down on us.

The entire town was abuzz with life, and for once, everything felt right. The loneliness that had plagued me just over a month ago was gone, and it all had to do with the demon who had chosen me.

My heart was full. Lighter.

It was too soon, wasn't it? A month was hardly enough time to get to know someone. Let alone to fall in love with them. And yet... I had.

I loved him.

Dammit, I'd fallen in love with my demon, all else be damned.

And I knew in my heart—I wanted him to stay. I didn't want this to end.

"Why?" I stopped, staring at the ground. "Why are you still here?" I'd avoided this conversation for too long. But I needed to hear it now. Needed to say the things I'd avoided out of fear of him leaving.

Because I wanted him to *stay*.

"You know why." He narrowed his eyes. "You can't tell me you don't feel this too. This thing between us."

"But..." I couldn't say that, because I *did* feel it. The golden thread, tied between us, that tether that was always pulling me to him. Like the fates had intertwined our lives together.

"Say it," he murmured. "It's the reason we can communicate with each other's minds. Why just being in your presence calms me. How everything always feels so right. There's a word for it between your people, too."

But there was a part of me that was scared to utter the words. Because if I did, that would make it *real*.

And if it was real, and he still chose to leave...

Then I'd be opening myself up for heartbreak. Because everyone always left me. Everyone but Luna. And even she'd chosen to move out instead of staying with me in our parents' old house.

But that string of fate... *Soulmates.*

We couldn't be. It wasn't *possible*. Right? I hadn't even believed in soulmates when we first met. The idea that there was someone out there meant for me felt like a truth that I couldn't deny, no matter how hard I tried. Not anymore.

There was a rightness when we were together, a peace I felt anytime I was in his arms.

Soulmates. It clicked in place. And I knew it was true. That this was *real*.

That I couldn't deny it anymore.

"You're..." I stared up at him in shock. "How is that possible? Demons don't have souls."

How could we be destined for each other? Of all the people the fates could have chosen for me... Why was it the demon who stood in front of me now?

How could it have been anyone else?

Damien frowned. "Where'd you get the idea that we don't have souls?"

"W-what?" I stuttered. "That's what they taught us growing up. Why you make deals to take our souls—"

He huffed out a response. "Whoever's been teaching you about demons needs to get their facts straight, little witch." My demon smoothed down my hair. "Your education has been thoroughly lacking."

Though he was right. The witches' deep hatred of demonkind had given me multiple pauses throughout our relationship.

Our *relationship*. Gods. We'd ignored the word, hadn't given it a term, but that's what we'd been doing all along, hadn't we?

I'd been falling in love with him, and I had hardly given him a label besides *roommate* or friend.

"Don't change the subject, Damien," I said, crossing my arms over my chest. I wanted to be giddy over this realization —the idea that we were fated for each other—but all I could see was doubts and fears. "This still doesn't make any sense."

Besides, he *was* leaving. It wasn't like this changed anything. I was mortal, and he would live hundreds more years. He had to go back to the demon realm. To the brother he served.

"You're—why not?"

"Do you really think anyone is going to believe it?"

"You're my mate, Willow." He cupped my cheeks. "The fates—they made you for me. It doesn't matter what anyone else thinks. Just what we think."

"But I'm nothing special. And you're..." I gestured at him. "You."

"Willow. Look at you." He cleared his throat. "I... I'm the one who's not worthy of you." He got down on his knees, dressed in his silly costume, holding both of my hands in his. "I've been in awe of you every single day since I first saw you. Your kindness, generosity... The way everyone loves you, because how could they not?" Damien shook his head. "You deserve better than me. But I want you, anyway. When I picture you with someone else, I want to tear them limb from limb. The thought of someone else touching you... No."

"Damien..." My heart stuttered in my chest. No one had ever said anything like that to me before. No one had ever made me feel so cared for—worshiped.

Even if this thing between us was the reason, if he only cared for me because we were mates, I still had him.

And I'd never felt so loved before.

Even if he hadn't said the words.

I hadn't either, after all.

After our little confession, we went to my cousin Cait's Halloween Party. She'd decked out the entire house, from lights and a fake skeleton on her porch to cobwebs hanging in every corner.

She popped out wearing a pair of fishnet tights, a ruffled top and a corset tied over her skirt. The bandana she'd tied around her forehead and her chunky jewelry just added to the pirate vibes.

"Willow!" Cait grinned, her orange hair glinting in the

light. "You made it!" She looked at my demon. "And you brought your man, too."

"You look incredible," I said, blushing at her comment. *My man.* It was true, but even then, it was still so new. "Thanks for inviting us."

"Of course! The rest of the girls are all here." Cait's familiar, a Russian blue cat, jumped on her shoulder, nuzzling at her cheek. "Hey, Thunder." She scratched underneath the cat's chin before it jumped down, coming to stand in front of Damien.

The gray cat sat, staring up at my demon, letting out a small meow.

Damien raised an eyebrow before bending down, holding out his hand. Thunder sniffed at his hand before brushing against it, back and forth, beginning to purr.

My cousin's eyes were wide. "He doesn't do this with anyone but me."

Damien rubbed the top of the cat's head before standing back up, sliding back against my side. "What can I say?" His voice was rough. "Cats love me."

Says the cat. I chuckled. Cait didn't know how loaded that statement was.

"This is nice," he murmured a few minutes later at my side, drinking a beer from a plastic cup. They'd gotten orange ones and doodled fake jack-o'-lantern faces on them. It made me smile seeing my demon holding something so silly.

"Sure," I agreed. "Until the coven descends."

"What?"

I raised an eyebrow. "Are you ready for the interrogation?"

Like clockwork, the other ten members of our coven appeared in front of us.

Rina. Wendy. The twins who ran the renovation and construction business, Tammy and Talley. Olive. Constance.

Celeste. Iris. Sophie. Gretchen. All witches of different shapes and sizes, a sea of different hair colors between them. Lavender, light blue, even neon green. And yet one thing united all of us. Our coven. The only one missing was Luna.

Cait stood sheepishly in the back. *Sorry,* she mouthed.

I shrugged. It was what our coven did. We had each other's backs, and they were going to make sure he had only the noblest of intentions.

As long as they didn't know what happened behind closed doors, I was fine with that. I wanted to keep my sex life private, thank you very much.

I loved all of them, but these girls could *gossip*.

"We heard you brought your man," Wendy offered, smiling as she sipped on her drink, her blonde hair bobbing with the motion. She'd worn a red costume with a hood, even carrying a broom along with her. "I'm Wendy," she told Damien.

He looked her up and down before turning to me. "The Good Witch?" We'd watched *Casper Meets Wendy* the other night.

I laughed. "It's a little on the nose, isn't it?"

He wiggled his, and I could almost see the motion of him in cat form, his whiskers moving.

Rina, standing at Wendy's side, just laughed. Her short brown bob somehow further complemented her tanned skin tone, as if she was striving to look as far from her namesake—Sabrina—as possible.

"Damien, this is my coven." I gave a small sigh as I gestured to all of them, giving him each of their names as he shook hands and said hello.

I had to give him credit for not turning and running at the sheer sight of them. Eleven witches would have made anyone nervous, but he just took it all in stride.

The rest of them launched into their questions.

Maybe I'd made a mistake keeping them away from him so far. I didn't think so, though. I was glad we'd had this month practically to ourselves. To get to know each other. For those feelings to grow naturally between us. Sure, we were *soulmates* —fated to be together before we'd even been born, but it was deeper than that.

And maybe I just enjoyed having him to myself.

"So, Damien, how long are you sticking around Pleasant Grove?" I heard Rina ask as I tuned back into the conversation. They'd all been rapid firing, and Damien had been answering all of their questions patiently.

He looked at me, an eyebrow raised. "I haven't exactly decided yet."

Maybe that was what triggered my fears. He was my soulmate, but he wouldn't stay?

"I think that's it for questions now." I tugged at his arm, pulling him away from the group. I didn't even apologize to my coven for leaving so abruptly.

"Can we talk?"

Damien nodded. Maybe he sensed the discontent I felt inside of me. The dread I felt at his eventual departure.

Maybe it was time we had that long overdue conversation. About what we *were* and my *feelings*. Luna was right. She always was.

I loved him, and he was leaving.

I loved him, and I hadn't told him.

"Wil. What's wrong?" I rubbed my thumb over her knuckles, back and forth, as we stood in the back-yard of her cousin's party.

I could feel the anxiety pulsing through her veins. I thought I'd reassured her earlier, but clearly it hadn't been enough.

"It's nothing. But it's just... been a month." She looked down at the ground, avoiding my eyesight.

"A month?" I raised an eyebrow. "What does that have to do with anything?"

Willow frowned. "You said you'd stay for a month."

Oh. I hadn't promised her any longer. "Fuck. Baby. That was before..." *Us.* Before I'd realized I was in love with her. Before everything had changed.

"Don't go. Please." Willow's green eyes filled with unshed tears, sparkling in the light. "I couldn't..." She swallowed roughly. "I couldn't bear it if you were gone."

"Willow..." I pulled her into my body, letting her bury her face in my chest as I flattened my palms against her back. "I'd never leave you, my little witch."

"You promise?" She looked up at me, and I almost dropped to my knees right there.

Fuck, but I loved her.

"With everything that I am, I'm yours." I kissed her forehead. "Forever."

She slumped against me, giving me her full weight. "I didn't want to lose you, but I felt so guilty asking you to stay, too." Her head stayed buried in my chest, her words slightly muffled through my t-shirt. "I know you have responsibilities and things, and that's your home, but..."

"You're my home now," I said, meaning it with every fiber of my being. "My mate." I kissed her forehead.

Willow pulled away, and I reached out to grab her wrist. There was still more I needed to say. Things I had to explain. "Listen, there's something I should tell you—"

"Have you seen Luna?" She interrupted, looking around with a frown on her face at her cousin's backyard, and then into the house. "She said she was going to meet us hours ago."

I shook my head. "Maybe something's keeping her?"

She whipped out her phone, sending a quick message to her sister. Pacing back and forth, she waited for a response.

It didn't come.

Worry crept into my veins.

"I'm going to try tracking her," she said, pressing a few more buttons on the screen. "It says she's... still at the bakery. But..."

"Why don't we go check on her?" I offered.

If it gave her the peace of mind, then that was worth it. Especially so we could get back to enjoying the festivities. Not that I cared one bit about spending time with the witches in town, but I knew what it meant to Willow. How much these people meant to her.

Luna was probably fine, in her apartment, getting ready. Or

maybe she'd chosen to make another batch of sweets at the bakery. I'd lost count of how many times my witch had come home with a box of something her sister had made.

Willow nodded, heading out the back fence. Following the streets to downtown, she pulled me towards their shop.

The windows were dark except for the soft glow of the lights strung across the counter. No one was inside. The whole place was silent.

"Maybe she's getting ready upstairs." Willow rushed around to the side door, rushing up the stairs two at a time. She reached for the handle, pausing to look at me. "It's... unlocked."

"Get behind me," I said. What if someone had broken in? Or were still inside?

But when I opened the door, Willow peeking around my arm, the apartment was deathly still. Dark. Quiet.

Empty.

We looked through all the rooms, but she was gone—without a trace—her cell phone sitting on the kitchen island.

Even her cat, Selene, wasn't there.

The bad feeling in my gut was slowly getting worse. If she wasn't here—in town—then there was only one place she could be. Which meant that...

I closed my eyes, detecting faint traces of two different smells in the apartment. Luna's, and... my brother's. Fuck.

"Damien. Where's my sister?" She looked around the apartment frantically. "What happened to her? And Selene..."

Both of them.

"I... *Shit.*" Shaking my head, I pinched the bridge of my nose. "I thought I had more time. He came early."

"What?"

"There's something I haven't told you." My eyes connected with hers, those beautiful green showing complete concern for her sister. And hurt. Because I hadn't let her in. "It's about my brother."

"*Where. Is. Luna*?" She emphasized each word with a pause, poking at my chest. "What are you not telling me?" Those green eyes that I loved narrowed.

I was glad she didn't have gifts of fire, or I would have worried about her burning the entire building down.

I grimaced, looking over at Willow. "I think maybe... my brother took her."

"Your... Brother." She stood frozen, perfectly still in the dim lighting of the apartment's kitchen. "The half brother, the fucking *Prince of Hell?* Why would he take my sister?"

"Not hell," I said, cursing internally. *Not the time.* "But yes, that's the one. He took her back to the demon realm to..." I didn't think my witch would appreciate the whole *make her his queen* thing. "You know how demons believe in mates?" *Like we are.*

Willow nodded. "Luna's always had a knack for setting people up. I never really believed in them until..." She trailed off. *You*, the implication was clear.

"Right. Well... I haven't told you everything about why I came to your world."

She cocked her head. "What?"

"Maybe you should sit down."

The anger in her eyes flared. "I don't want to sit down. I want my *baby* sister to be sitting on her couch, safe and sound. Not in the *fucking demon realm*!"

"I know."

"She's my little sister, Damien. I was supposed to protect her. Make sure she was okay." Her voice choked up as she finally slumped onto the couch. "I can't believe your brother would kidnap her."

"He believes that, well..." I shook my head. "That she's *his* fated mate."

Surprise, Willow, I thought to myself bitterly. *My brother's a giant asshole who couldn't keep his filthy paws off your sister!*

Yeah, I was royally screwed.

"Luna?" Her jaw dropped open. "Like... he wants to..." Her brain must have been running a million miles an hour. "How long have you known about this?"

I sighed, sinking onto the floor next to her. "A while. It's why I was here."

"In Pleasant Grove?"

I nodded. Whatever had called me here when I was still in cat form, it had been right. "And the human realm. He sent me to look for her."

"And you found..." *Me.*

"Yes. Finding you, Willow... That was the happiest coincidence of my life. But I never thought Zain would be looking for your sister."

"Why didn't you tell me?" Her voice was almost a whimper. "We could have done something. Stopped this."

I shook my head. "I didn't want to lose you. And if he made me go back—"

"But now I've lost her, Damien. She's my only family. My best friend."

I pulled her into my arms as the first tears fell, holding her upright so she didn't fall onto the floor. "I know, baby. I know."

I held her as she cried in my arms, rubbing a soothing hand over her back.

"We'll get her back," I promised. "We can go tonight."

She blinked. "To the Demon Realm?"

Yes. I offered her my hand, pulling her off from the couch.

"We'll go make sure she's okay. No harm will come to her, I promise you that."

Okay. Her sweet voice slipped into my mind, clutching my hand tight.

I brushed away her tears with my free hand, rubbing over her jawbone with my thumb.

I'm so sorry, I murmured into her mind.

Leading her back down the stairs, I moved to the back alley. The same one I'd opened a portal in weeks ago. The day I'd realized who Luna was.

I was thankful that most everyone in the town was currently in the town square, or milling about downtown, because no one was back here to witness this.

Opening up a portal, I commanded the shadows to do my bidding.

"Are you sure this is a good idea?" Willow murmured, clutching onto my arm as I commanded the shadows to open a portal to my brother. "Me going there?" Her eyes were still red, and full of worry. "What about the demons?"

"I'll protect you, I promise."

"I know." Her voice didn't falter. "I'm *really* pissed at you, but I know you will." Her hand slid up my chest. "Now, let's go get my sister."

I nodded.

"Hold on tight," I instructed her, curling my arm around her wrist to hold her tight to me.

And we stepped through the darkness.

"This is... nothing like what I expected." Willow's eyes trailed over the outside of the palace, catching on all the ornate details. The polished stone shone, even with the moon high in the sky.

"What did you expect?"

"Hm. Darker. More black and red." She looked up at the sky. "An endless darkness. Blood. I don't know. Stuff like that."

"Ah." I couldn't exactly fault her for that.

I'd grown up here, so the gray palace walls didn't phase me, but I could see how they might have differed from what she expected.

The palace itself rivaled any in the human world, that much I knew. It was lavish—unrivaled in its magnificence.

"What do I call him?"

"Him?"

"Your brother."

"Ah. Well, Zain would prefer *Your Majesty* or *Your Highness,* I'm sure. But you can just call him his given name. That's what I do." I flashed her a grin. "You're not his citizen. He can't touch you."

"I've never met royalty before," she said, tugging down her dress.

I couldn't help but laugh when I realized we were still wearing our Halloween costumes. She really looked like a witch in her garb. Thankfully, we didn't stand out very much in them around here. The demon realm fashions hadn't changed too much over the last few centuries.

"What?" she asked, tilting her head at my chuckle.

"You realize *I'm* a prince as well, right?"

"Oh." Willow flushed. "Well..." She looked at me out of the corner of her eye. "You're different."

"Why?" I paused, tugging on her arm to bring her face to face with me. "What if I wanted you to call me *Your Majesty?*"

"Damien," she groaned, her cheeks growing even pinker. "That's not who you are to me. You're just..."

"Just what?"

My Damien.

I kissed her cheek before I guided her in through the palace doors, nodding to the guards standing at attention. *I like that even better, little witch.*

I thought you might, came her response.

The throne room's just ahead. I could feel her trembling, so I tightened my grip on her hand to reassure her. *I've got you.*

She tried to force her face into a smile, but even that couldn't mask the worry I felt pulsing through her body. *I know.*

Zain sat on his throne. Cool, calm—too calm.

"Ah, Damien. How nice to see you! I see you brought your witch."

I bared my teeth. "Where is she?"

"Who?" He cocked his head.

"My sister," Willow said, narrowing her eyes.

"Ah." Zain gave a lazy smile. "She's right here. Come on out, moonbeam." Luna walked out next to my brother, dressed in a white gossamer gown—looking pale, but not in anguish like I might have expected.

Willow choked out a sob. "Oh, thank god."

My brother whispered something into Luna's ear, and then she was down the stairs—colliding into Willow's arms for a hug.

"Are you okay?" Willow tightened her arms around her sister, like if she held tight enough, she could pretend this never happened. But it had. And it was my fault. I could have prevented all of it.

"Brother." I turned to him, face stone cold as I stepped up in front of him. "We had an agreement."

He rolled his eyes, somehow managing to look both annoyed and amused. "We had no such thing."

"I said—"

Zain shook his head. "Damien. I don't want to fight. I..." His eyes slid over to Luna, and for the first time, there seemed to be a sparkle there.

"She's her *sister*, Zain." I spat the words.

A sliver of remorse showed on his face, only for a moment. "And you're..." He looked between my witch and I.

"Yes. Willow's my mate." I chuckled. "Funny that you sent me to find *your* Queen, and it led to me finding mine as well."

He raised his eyebrows and said, "You're not planning on returning, are you?"

My muscles tensed. I wanted to stay with Willow, but I still had a vow to my brother. And yet...

"No. I want to stay with her."

"You love her."

I nodded. "Yes." With everything I was. Even if I hadn't told her that yet. I hadn't earned hearing the words from her lips. Not yet.

"Will you be staying, brother? I'd love to get to know your mate."

"I don't—"

We cut our conversation short as Willow came back to my side, sliding her arm around my waist. I wanted to bury my head in her hair, inhaling her scent. She looked up at me, and then back to her sister.

Should we go? I asked her.

Not without Luna, she replied, her voice sweet in my mind.

Of course. I nodded at my mate.

"Let's go home, Luna," Willow said, offering a hand to her sister.

But Luna shook her head, looking over at my brother. "I..." She walked back to Zain's side, standing next to him in front of the throne.

182

Let my brother take her hand in his.

"I know it's crazy, Wil," Luna told her sister. "But... I feel like I have to do this. To see where it goes."

"Are you sure?"

Luna nodded, the action loosening her blonde curls, bringing them down over the silky white dress. All she needed was a tiara, and she would look like a princess. "I want to do this. We made a deal."

Willow's gasp echoed through the hall. What had they bargained for?

I wasn't sure I wanted to know.

"We're having a ball tonight," my brother announced. "You two are welcome to attend if you want to stay. I'll be announcing my betrothal to my *fiancee.*"

That was when I noticed the gemstone that sat on Luna's ring finger.

Willow's eyes darted to her sister.

She's really going to do it, Willow thought bitterly. *She said* yes.

It's her choice, little witch.

I know, it's just—

"Well?"

Willow's face smoothed out into a pleasant smile. Anything to hide the thoughts I felt warring in her mind. "We'd love to attend your ball, Prince Zain."

His face flattened out into a smooth smile. "Brother?"

"My witch's will is my command," I promised. I'd stay by her side, no matter what. Wherever she wanted to be; wherever she wanted to go—I'd be there. "I live to fulfill her every wish."

Zain's face curled up into a knowing smirk. *Whipped already, brother?* His face seemed to say.

183

If only he knew the half of it. How far gone I was for her. How much I loved her.

"We'll see you tonight then," he said.

What had we just gotten ourselves into? And what the hell had I been thinking, bringing her here? I *hadn't*.

It was just that she'd been so concerned about Luna, and I wanted to make sure she was okay. That Luna wasn't being kept against her will.

And now, I'd roped us into a party where hundreds, if not thousands, of demons would be present.

Instead of being safe and comfortable in Willow's house, enjoying the rest of her favorite holiday.

"Let's go to my rooms, little witch," I murmured into her ear.

At least we'd be safe there.

willow

There was a first time for everything, and mine was attending a freaking *ball* in *Hell*. Okay, the demon realm might not have exactly been what I imagined, but I'd never pictured *this*.

Especially not the plush *giant* bed with the softest pillows I'd ever laid my head on.

"I'm never leaving this bed ever again," I groaned, laying out like a starfish and closing my eyes as I sunk into the mattress. It still smelled faintly of my demon, even if he'd been occupying my bed for the last few weeks instead of his own. I inhaled that spicy smell, loving the way it invaded my senses.

When I opened them, it was to a pair of red eyes looking down into mine. Damien had perched himself over top of me, his lips curled up into a smirk. "I'd be okay with that," he purred.

"Hm?"

"You never leaving my bed." He leaned down, pressing a kiss to my forehead.

I stretched my arms out, moving my hands in a grabby motion. "Come here."

He climbed on top of me, pinning me in place with his powerful arms.

"Are you still mad at me?"

"A little." I sighed, running my hands over the slight stubble on his jaw. I wondered what it would be like if he let it grow out. He'd kept his face and neck shaved so far, but... what about the future? "Mostly that you didn't tell me."

"I should have. But I didn't know how to tell you without telling you that you were my mate, and that was why I couldn't let you go. Couldn't leave you."

I leaned up to press a soft kiss against his lips. "I understand."

"You do?"

Nodding, I closed my eyes for a moment. "I was scared, too. That if I told you how I felt, you'd still leave."

"Never." He kissed my cheek. "You know that now, right?"

I nodded. "Yes."

The heat was pooling in my veins from the way he held his body over top of me, a desire for him to pin me down, to feel that delicious weight over mine.

"Damien," I mumbled. "What are you doing?"

"Earning my forgiveness." Kissing my neck, he worked his way up till he found my lips. "While I'd love to take my time with you—" he paused to kiss the side of my lips, "I'd need all night—" another kiss to the other side. "And we have to get ready for the party."

"Mmm." I pouted as he interlocked our lips once more before pulling away. "Not fair."

Damien gave me a little smirk before getting off the bed, pulling me up into a sitting position. "Tonight," he promised. And I knew in my heart that I'd already forgiven him. Luna was safe. He'd brought me here to give me that peace of mine. And I loved him. So much.

I heaved a sigh. "Fine."

"Besides, don't you want to see your dress?"

Perking up, I repeated, "My dress?"

He nodded. "Mhm."

Quirking an eyebrow, I clambered off the bed. "When did you have time to get me a dress?"

Damien's lips curled into a small smile as he took my hand. "I have my ways."

He tugged me into the giant dressing rooms that adjoined his room, and the sound of the door closing behind us echoed off the walls.

My jaw dropped as I saw what was hanging on the rack.

They'd detailed the dress with hundreds of tiny diamonds, which made it sparkle like the stars in the night sky. The midnight blue color blended into a deep purple as it rippled to the floor. Even more crystals detailed the sweetheart neckline of the silky gown.

"Oh. Damien." I gasped. "It's beautiful." Spinning around, I threw my arms around his neck, bringing my lips to his. "Thank you. I love it." Giggling, I kissed him again.

I love you. The words were on the tip of my tongue. But I swallowed them down. Even if he said he wouldn't leave, that he'd stay with me... Admitting how I felt still scared me.

What if it was still too soon? I swallowed it down, refocusing on my demon's handsome face. I traced his jaw with my hand.

He nuzzled his nose against mine. "Do you want to take a bath before we get ready?"

My eyes lit up. "Together?"

Damien laughed. "Little witch. You're going to kill me." He kissed the side of my cheek. Whispered in my ear. "If we get in there together, we're not getting out. Not until you're covered in my scent and look freshly fucked, so everyone knows exactly whose you are."

"Yours," I said, burying my face in his throat. Inhaling his smell like he always did mine. "I'm yours."

He kissed me one more time, his tongue slipping into my mouth as I let out a contented sigh. I didn't want to let go, but Damien set me down, guiding me into the lavish bathroom.

After two lesser demons who appeared from nowhere had cleaned and pampered me, my hair was curled and they tied me into my gown.

The soft silky fabric was smooth against my fingers, slipping through like liquid metal.

"Wow." Damien's voice brought me out of my trance. When I looked up, I was struck by the sight of him in a stunning tuxedo. "Just... Wow."

I blushed.

"You look incredible, Willow." His voice choked up, speechless.

"You look pretty great yourself, demon." I tugged on his lapel.

He pulled away before I could kiss him, his thumb rubbing over the sparkles they'd brushed onto my cheeks. Like he knew what I wanted.

"Shall we?" He offered me an arm, and I slid mine into his.

"Yes."

And my *mate* took me to the first ball of my life.

I glanced back and forth, trying to get a glimpse of my sister.

"Relax," Damien murmured into my ear, running his hand down my spine. "I'm sure she's okay."

"I know, but..."

We didn't get to talk properly earlier. Away from prying eyes and ears.

I was sure I could trust Damien, but his brother?

There were waiters making their way through the crowded ballroom, dressed in simple black suits, distracting from their innate demon-ness. Some of them had horns, or solid black eyes that felt like they could stare right through you. There were even beings with dark black feathered wings and some with barbed tails.

"They'll want to make a grand entrance, most likely," he said as he handed me a glass of a shimmering gold liquid.

"What is this?" I asked, swirling it around.

"Demon wine."

I blinked at him. *What?*

"Just try it," he encouraged, picking up a flute of his own. "You'll like it. It's sweet."

I took a sip, and—*woah*. I'd never tasted anything like it. All the regular wine paled in comparison to the smooth liquid sliding down my throat. "*Oh*."

"Don't drink too much of it. Gives you a bitch of a hangover." He chuckled.

I giggled, taking another drink. "It's good." My head was already feeling light after just a few sips of the drink. It would be too easy to get drunk off of it.

Another waiter passed by us, this time with a tray of food, multiple pairs of horns curling away from his forehead. A thought popped into my head.

I looked up at Damien. "What do you really look like?"

"What do you mean?" He raised a dark eyebrow.

I squinted my eyes. "Isn't this form of yours some sort of glamor? To look like a human?" If so, he'd accomplished it. The

189

only feature on him that wasn't human-like were those piercing red eyes.

"What are you expecting?" He scoffed. "Cat ears? A tail?"

I shrugged. "I don't know. You don't have horns?" I poked at his forehead, where his dark black hair rested.

He laughed. "No. My dad does, but my mom was a regular shifter. I got her features." Damien wrapped an arm around my waist, pulling our bodies against each other's. "Why? Do you like the horns, baby?"

I shook my head, sliding a hand against the side of his face. "I like you just the way you are."

But I'm not saying no to the cat ears, either.

He laughed, brushing his lips over my pulse point, the tip of his tooth brushing over my skin. "You're cute."

Taking another sip of my wine, I couldn't help my smile.

"Look!" I exclaimed suddenly, catching a blur of white in the corner of my eye. "They're here."

The ballroom practically came to a standstill as Zain came to the top of the stairs, my sister standing at his side. The demon holding my sister's hand was not what I expected when I thought of Damien's brother.

Damien and him looked almost identical with their jet black hair, sharp nose, and chiseled jawline, but there was a distinct difference in his presence.

Zain was less rugged, and more... *Princely.* His whole demeanor screamed royalty. He was handsome, perfectly polished, and just as tall as my demon, but in the place of Damien's blood-red eyes sat two golden ones. They were almost piercing, and though I'd always thought of gold as a warm color, his gaze felt cold.

Until it fell upon my sister, and I saw some of that cold facade melting away.

Huh.

"Now presenting, the Crown Prince and his fiancée, our Princess-to-be. Prince Zain and Lady Luna!" The room erupted into cheers as the demon finished his proclamation, stepping back into the shadows.

Luna, at his side, was wearing a ballgown that looked like hundreds of tiny stars interwoven together, and every time she caught the light, she sparkled. It was gorgeous—she was impossible to take your eyes off of. When you combined it with the tiara of crystals sitting on her head, she looked every bit the title she was about to undertake.

Princess of the Demons. I shook my head. I still had no idea what she was thinking.

They glided down the stairs, heading towards the front of the ballroom together.

Finishing my flute of wine, I turned to Damien, ready to go talk to Luna, but a voice interrupted me.

"Who's this pretty little thing you have with you, Damien?"

My demon stiffened, his arm coming around my front. Guarding me against whatever danger he thought this male posed.

Could other demons sense a mating bond? Ours was still so new—precious, precariously settled between us. And how had I not realized it sooner? Now that I knew, it was so obvious.

With my magic, I could see the gold threads that intertwined between us. There was no doubt in my mind that they'd grow stronger—thicker—with time.

The demon gave him an evil grin, one that instantly made my stomach drop. "Did you bring us a new plaything, *Prince?*" He said the last word with a sneer. Unlike Damien, who appeared mostly human, this demon wore his true form—

horns curving up his forehead, and a sickly gray pallor to his skin.

My jaw dropped. Even though Damien had told me about how he did Zain's bidding, I couldn't believe people talked about him like this.

"How dare you—" I started, but my demon tugged me tighter against him. This demon should have been terrifying, and yet—I felt perfectly safe. Because I knew he would protect me.

Damien growled, practically guarding me with his body. "She's *mine*." His lips curled up over his teeth, and I could see the exposed fangs there. "No one else will ever touch her except me." You could hear the snarl in his voice. "And if anyone tries, they'll find out exactly how it feels to really be in *Hell*." His red eyes were smoldering, like fire inside his irises as he turned back to me.

The other demon backed away slightly, holding up his hands in surrender.

I frowned, tugging at his jacket to bring his face into view. "Why do they talk to you like that? You're a prince too."

He sighed. "I'm the bastard son of the King. They've never let me forget it."

"Oh." I ran my fingers through his hair. "Do you really think they'd try to hurt me?"

He shook his head. "I would never risk finding out." I felt weightless as he scooped me up into his arms and carried me away.

"Damien," I murmured, rubbing my hand over his jaw. "You don't have to do this."

"What?" He spoke through clenched teeth.

"Try to protect me." I leaned in, nibbling on his ear. "I'm a big girl. I can protect myself." I wiggled my fingers. "Witch, remember?" A few sparks emitted from my fingertips.

"You're so little," he muttered. "Fragile. I don't... I can't... My instincts are going crazy right now." He sighed in frustration, setting me down in a dark corner before rubbing his face against my throat.

"What are you doing?" I laughed.

"Trying to make you smell like me."

I raised an eyebrow. "What?"

"If you smell like me, the other demons will leave you alone. Know that you're mine."

"And..." I swallowed. "That's the best way to do it?"

His eyes connected with mine, and he gave a slow shake of his head as his fangs popped out of his lips. "No."

Heat flared in his eyes, his voice like gravel, rasping out. "There's another way. But I don't want to hurt you, Wil." His thumb brushed over my cheek.

"You can't." I shook my head. "You won't." I believed in him fully. I knew that no matter what happened, he would protect me.

"You don't understand. If I claim you, I could lose control. My demon senses would take over."

He cupped my face, and I closed my eyes, leaning into his warm palm. "It's okay, Damien. I trust you. I... want you to claim me." My cheeks flushed with warmth. "Please." My voice was a whisper in the night.

Shadows had fallen all around us, like a comfortable blanket, but I didn't mind. I knew they were his doing. That they were keeping us wrapped up in each other, even in the middle of the busy ballroom.

"Willow, I..." His lips crashed against mine. "Fuck."

I was lost in the moment as he kissed me, his breath mingling with mine. The kiss was rough, but I couldn't get enough as he claimed my mouth again and again.

His fangs brushed against my bottom lip, and I moaned

from the sensation, even as his tongue explored every inch of my mouth.

My body was on fire, alight from every little touch. I whimpered softly as the sensation washed over me.

It was too much. It wasn't enough.

"Gonna take you here, so they all know that you're mine." His lips connected with my neck, kissing a line down to my chest. "Claim my pretty mate in public, hm?"

I whimpered. "Damien..."

I knew the dark surrounded us, but even the idea that someone could see us—even in a place like this, full of demons —shouldn't have turned me on more, but somehow, it did. When his fingers trailed over my slit, I knew exactly what he'd find. I was soaking wet. Thank the Goddess there was a slit in my ballgown, giving him access.

"My little witch. So good for me," he murmured against my neck as he pushed my lace panties aside. "So wet."

I moaned, baring my neck to him further.

He sank his teeth into me, those fangs piercing the skin of my throat. I'd expected pain, but pure pleasure exploded across the bite, and I moaned deeply from the sensation.

"Fuck, Willow," he groaned. "You taste so good." He didn't drink from me, but the claiming bite tingled, ripples of ecstasy flowing through my body.

"Damien. Please." I mewled, needing more. "I need—"

He dipped his fingers inside of me, working me higher while his tongue gently brushed against my bite. With each stroke of his tongue over the teeth marks, my body trembled with pleasure.

"I've got you, baby," he soothed. "My mate. My beautiful mate."

The moment his thumb connected with my clit, I slumped against him, my knees going weak.

"You need to come, hm?"

"Y-yes." I buried my face in his neck, inhaling his spicy scent.

"What do you want?" He asked, crooking his fingers inside of me. "My fingers or my cock?"

Inside me, I begged, hardly coherent enough to know if I'd said the words out loud or not. I didn't care that we were up against a wall, with the only thing keeping anyone from seeing us being Damien's shadows.

I longed for him, knowing that only his presence could ease the burning sensation inside of me. Damien's playful fingers kept teasing me while my dress remained bunched up around my waist, and I clung to him.

"You're going to have to be quiet, little witch." He rumbled against my ear, his breath tickling my skin. "My shadows will keep anyone from seeing us, but I can't say the same thing about them *hearing* us."

Were we about to fuck in the middle of the crowded ballroom? *Yes.*

I nodded in agreement as Damien unzipped his pants, pulling himself out, revealing his hardening length to me. If we were somewhere else, I would have dropped to my knees right there and begged to taste him.

But this fire in me, this burning, maddening emptiness, wasn't going away without help. Only his touch could soothe it. Was that the mating bond? Did demons feel this too?

Fisting his cock, he roughly tugged on it a few times before bringing his tip to my entrance, running it through my wetness.

Teasing me, over and over, without letting the tip slip inside.

Please.

Are you gonna be quiet, baby?

Yes. I nodded into his jacket. *Now fuck me.*

I didn't care about anything else as he finally pushed inside of me, burying himself to the hilt. Neither of us said a word as he braced us against a wall, giving it to me with everything he had. Damien wrapped his free hand—the one not currently holding me in place against him—over my mouth, keeping me from making a sound.

We both lost ourselves in the sensation as he drove us higher and higher. His shadows joined in, a cool press against my skin, and I was *gone.*

Exploding, just like that.

He wasn't far behind me, and I squeezed my insides around him, feeling him growing even harder inside.

"Willow," he groaned as he came, spilling rope after rope of cum inside of me.

Every warring emotion inside me calmed as the warmth spread through my insides, leaving me feeling peaceful and content. It was like a balm to my soul, and I felt the beast within me finally relax and let go. Damien placed a kiss on my lips before pulling out, re-situating my underwear in place before letting my dress fall back down to the ground.

"Damien," I whispered as I took a step, fully aware of the way the shadows were dissipating from around us.

"What, baby?"

Grabbing my hand, he interlaced our fingers, giving me a guilty smile.

"Your cum is dripping out of me."

He flashed me a devilish smile as his shadows danced up my thighs before pushing it back inside of me. "I know." Leaning into my ear, he said to me, "At least you smell like me now."

I hummed in response, still not having enough words for what we'd just done.

And how much I'd *liked it.*
Loved it, even.
Like I loved him.

TWENTY-TWO

"Luna!" I exclaimed, finally coming within an arm's reach of my sister for the first time all night.

She was so popular with the demons, I'd barely been able to keep track of her all night. Plus, when you added Damien thoroughly distracting me with that show in the shadows... this was my first opportunity to actually talk to her.

When I made it to her side, I instantly wrapped my arms around her, hugging her tight before pulling away.

Her dress was even more intricate and beautiful now that I was seeing it close up. It sparkled every time it caught the light under the chandeliers. "Wow. This is beautiful." She exuded an air of elegance, with every detail on her expertly curated. Not a strand of hair was out of place, and her makeup was flawlessly applied. The work of demons, I was sure.

"Thank you." She messed with the skirts. "Did Damien give you yours?"

I nodded. I still had no idea how he'd been able to procure it in time.

But that wasn't what was important.

I just wanted to spend the little time I had with my sister talking about her. To know what was going on inside her head.

"Can we talk?" I asked, pointing to the outside balcony with my head. My hand was occupied with another glass of the sparkly gold beverage. I was a little addicted.

Luna nodded.

The breeze was cool against my balmy skin as we stepped out into the night. Luna rested against the railing as I propped my arms against it, looking out. "This place is... Wow. Definitely not in Pleasant Grove anymore."

"Mhm," she agreed.

"Luna." My voice was stern. "Talk to me."

She turned, looking into my eyes as she emitted a deep sigh. "I am, aren't I?"

I sighed. "You were right."

"About what?"

"Damien. Telling him how I felt."

"And you told him you love him?"

"Er... Well... No." My cheeks went pink. "I only realized that *today*."

"*Willow.*"

"Hey. Don't sister me while I'm sistering *you*." I crossed my arms over my chest. "Are you sure this is what you want?"

"So, you get to fall in love with a demon and be with him, but I can't?"

"Do you?" I asked softly. "Love him?"

Luna shook her head. "No." It was a whisper of an omission. "But..." When her eyes connected with mine, they were watery. "I can't explain it, Wil. But when I saw him, my heart knew."

"Knew...?"

"That he was mine. That I was his." She used her hands to

indicate everything around us. "Maybe I'm supposed to be *here*, you know?"

"But... Your bakery. Our lives. You're leaving everything behind."

She fidgeted with the ring that sat on her finger. "Lately, I've been thinking, well... I don't know how to describe it. Like I was missing something. And when he asked me to come with him, I didn't even have to stop to think about it. I just... said yes."

"But he's a stranger. You don't even know him."

Luna blinked. "Well... That's not entirely true."

"What?"

But... Damien had told me he'd been sent to the human world to find her. When would Zain have had the time to meet her?

"We've met before. At the bar." She shrugged. "And a few other times."

"You didn't think to tell me you *met someone?*" I dropped my voice, hoping she couldn't hear the hurt. "I'm your sister, Luna."

She sighed. "I know. But you were all wrapped up in Damien, and I didn't want to pop your bubble. Plus, it's not like you were one hundred percent truthful with me, either."

"Right. Well, *maybe* I should have told you about his, er... *demon-ness*. In my defense, I thought I was doing the right thing. Keeping him safe." I didn't think I'd needed to keep her safe too.

Luna laughed. "I don't think he needs you for that." She staring off into the distance at the palace gardens, the silence growing between us.

"A witch cursed him," I offered. "That's the spell I did. Reversing it."

"I thought I would hate it here," she admitted. "This place.

I thought it would be *hell*. But it's not. People are free to be whoever they are here. Monster and demon alike. It's nothing like Pleasant Grove."

"No, it isn't," I murmured. The moon was high in the sky, and the sky was scattered with stars—constellations I didn't know, didn't have the names for.

Luna picked up my hand, squeezing it tightly. "I don't know what will happen, but I can promise you I'm safe here. I'm not here against my will. I chose this... I choose *him*."

"Okay," I whispered, squeezing back. "And if you decide this isn't what you want anymore?"

"Then I'll come back."

Back, she said. Not home. Because maybe Pleasant Grove wasn't her home anymore. Not when her soulmate was here.

"Okay," I agreed as we dropped hands, still staring out at the palace's surroundings. I still couldn't believe a place like this could exist in the demon realm. How much that we'd been taught was wrong.

But maybe... hiding Damien had never been the right thing to do from the beginning. Maybe I needed to show the other witches that demons weren't all bad. That they were capable of love. Life.

"There you two are," Zain said, wrapping an arm around Luna's shoulders. "We've been looking for you."

Damien stepped to my side, and I instantly wanted to bury myself in his warmth. It hadn't been that long since he'd touched me last, but I'd already missed it.

"Hi," I murmured, slipping an arm around his middle.

"We were just getting some air," Luna responded. "It's a little stuffy in there." She tugged at one sleeve of her dress.

My sister's demon prince—her *fiancé*, I had to remind myself—chuckled. "They're just fascinated by you, my bride. Give it time." He kissed her cheek.

I was surprised at how tender and loving he seemed to be. Was it all an act?

She sighed. "I know."

He turned his attention to Damien and I. "Did you two enjoy the party?"

"Oh, yes," I said, thinking about the demon wine. Definitely not what we'd done in the shadows. "It's been lovely."

Zain laughed, turning his attention to his brother. "She smells like you now."

My cheeks were on fire, like he'd caught us red-handed, and Damien nuzzled his nose against my neck.

"I had to keep the other demons away from my mate somehow."

Zain looked down at Luna, humming slightly in response.

"I can take care of myself," she muttered, rolling her eyes as she stared out at the gardens.

Sounds a lot like someone else I know, Damien muttered into my mind.

Shut it. I'm pretty sure your brother knows what we did earlier.

So?

So, I'm mortified.

He laughed. *So you don't want to do it again?*

I narrowed my eyes at him. "I didn't say that."

Luna raised an eyebrow at me, but I just shook my head.

I'd have time in the future where I could explain our weird telepathy thing to her. Who knows, maybe she had it too? We hadn't exactly had a lot of time to compare our *demons* with each other.

Resting my head against Damien's chest, I shivered. The cool air had felt nice before, but now it was getting chillier.

Plus, I was exhausted. I'd been up since this morning, and Halloween felt like yesterday. It was weird to remind myself that it had been tonight. It must have been close to two in the morning already.

He scooped me up into his arms for the second time tonight. "Come on, my mate. Let's get you to bed."

I yawned. Nothing sounded better.

"Goodnight, you two," Luna said, offering me a smile.

I gave her a wave. "Night." I looked at Zain. "Don't hurt my baby sister, or I'll tear your heart out." I looked at Damien. "Or turn you into a cat. Might be just as effective."

My demon laughed. "I think you had too much demon wine, baby."

"Uh-uh," I argued, feeling myself get sleepier as we walked away. But it was hard to deny the fact when I'd had a glass in my hand most of the night. I didn't feel drunk, though. Just a warm, pleasant buzz.

"Sleep, little witch," he soothed. "We'll talk more in the morning."

I nodded into his chest.

Yes. In the morning, I'd tell him everything I'd left unsaid.

Starting with those three words.

Stretching my arms, I sat up, clutching the sheet around my naked body. Damien was sprawled out at my side, one arm possessively over my stomach.

I'd passed out in his arms the night before as he carried me. He roused me from my half-sleep to help me out of my dress before we took a brief shower together. The day had left me feeling completely depleted.

I watched him sleep, curling my fingers through his dark hair.

"I'm so glad I adopted you," I murmured. "Thanks for being my not-cat, Demon."

He stirred at my touch, grabbing my hand and kissing my knuckles as he woke.

"Good morning, Willow," he said, voice groggy from sleep. But he didn't give me my arm back—no, he placed gentle kisses all the way up my arm before pausing at the mark he'd left yesterday on my neck.

"I like my mark on you." The sound of his voice was like a deep, rumbling growl. "Fuck. What it does to me..." He kissed the mark before tracing his tongue over it.

"Damien." I ran my fingers through his hair once more. "I need to tell you something—"

"I still owe you a favor, you know."

I kissed him to shut him up. "You *are* my favor, demon."

He laughed against my mouth.

I sat up, not caring about bringing the sheet with me. "I mean it. You... I never could have imagined this. You. Us. And I l—"

He shook his head. "Don't say it. Not yet." The fangs popped out from his upper lip. *I want to say it first.*

I shook my head, even though I loved his possessiveness. "Why did you stay?" I let the words slip out. I'd asked him something similar before, but this time, it was different. "Besides me being your mate."

"Isn't it obvious?"

"Maybe I need to hear it. The words."

"Willow." Damien's forehead rested against mine. "I stayed for *you*, little witch. Because I couldn't bear to be apart from you. Because you're mine." The corner of his lip tilted up, exposing a canine tooth. "I've never had somebody of my own. Somebody to..." His voice choked up. "Love."

"You...?" My eyes filled with tears. Maybe I'd thought it was too soon to say the words myself. Even then, I'd been seconds away admitting the same thing to him. How could I not, after letting him claim me yesterday? My fingers fluttered up to the bite, tracing the puncture wounds.

"I love you." He took my hands in his, intertwining our fingers together. I marveled at how perfectly we fit, just like always. "I think I've loved you since I first laid eyes on you, Willow."

"But you..." My eyes widened. *You were a cat.*

Damien sucked in a breath. Nodded. I didn't need to say the words, because he knew what I was thinking. Our bond gave us that, always. "Even then, I think I knew what you were to me. But it wasn't until you helped me get back into this form that I *knew*. But it's more than that."

I blinked. "It is?"

"You're *mine*, but that's not why I fell in love with you, little witch." He brushed his fingers over my chin. "I fell in love with you because you're clever, and kind, and you never give up on people." Damien gave me a small smile. "Especially not on me. And I've never had anything that was mine before. Really, truly *mine*. Never had somewhere that felt like home before you. But fuck, Willow. I'd give up anything for you. Do anything for you. Burn down hell just for a chance—just for a moment with you."

"I love you too," I said, unable to contain all of the emotions flowing through me. "I have for a while. I wanted to tell you, but I was just... scared."

"Of what?" Tucking a strand of hair behind my ear, gently, he looked more vulnerable than I'd ever seen him before. More open, too. "I'd never leave you."

"I know that now." I sighed, burying my head against his pecs. "But before... I thought you'd have to go back here. That you wouldn't be able to stay."

"You were something I never expected, never hoped for, but... I'd never trade you for the world, Willow. My mate," he murmured. "My beautiful mate."

"Damien..." My eyes filled with tears. "I love you. So much." I wrapped my arms around him, letting our lips connect.

Kissing the man I loved.

Kissing the man who loved *me.*

"Do you want to go home?" He tilted his head up to look at me, pausing all of the little touches I loved. I wanted them— craved *him,* but there were more important things right now.

"You don't want to... stay?" I asked, surprised. We had each other, but I hadn't known what our plans were. If he'd have to stay here, because of his brother. "This is your home." I would have hated every minute of it, even if he'd asked me to stay with him. But I would have understood. Even more so after Luna had decided to marry his brother.

He shook his head. "This isn't my home."

"What?" I laughed. "Isn't it?" I gestured to the room around us. These giant suites we'd occupied for only a night.

He cocked his head to the side. "That's not what I meant."

"Oh."

"I do though. Have my own house, away from the palace." He laid his head on my lap. "I'll take you there sometime."

I traced a finger over his jaw. "I'd love that."

"You're my home, Willow," he said, taking my hands in his. "I told you that. And wherever you want to be... I want to be there, too."

"Okay." I liked the sound of that.

"Home?" He asked again, his voice quiet.

"Home," I agreed.

·· ✦ ☽ ☀ ☾ ✦ ··

After we'd finally extracted ourselves from the bed, washing up in the giant bathtub once again, we'd put on fresh clothes. I didn't ask where he'd gotten my clothes from. How his magic worked, exactly.

"I'm sorry," he offered as we walked back outside of the palace. Despite my initial reservations of the place, I was surprised how beautiful it was.

Damien and I had talked about Luna earlier while we were getting ready. My conversation with her.

"It's hard to rescue someone who doesn't want to be rescued." But if she wanted to be here—if she would be happy—then I'd let her go.

"No." He took my hand. "I mean, for not telling you. I should have told you that Luna was destined. That my brother would come for her. I'd spent weeks trying to figure out how to get around it. But..."

"I know." I cupped his cheek with my palm. "But as long as she wants to be there, then... It's her choice. She's an adult. If she wants to be with her..." My voice choked on the words. "*Fated mate,* then who am I to say anything? After all, I found you."

"Willow..."

My body tensed. "He won't hurt her, right?"

"No. Fuck. No, never." He took my hands in his. "He might be the heir to the demon throne, but he'd... He'd never harm your sister. Or force her to do anything she didn't want to do."

"Okay." I paused, looking back at the glittering tops of the palace. "We can come back, right?"

"Any time you want."

Still holding hands, I watched as Damien opened a portal back to my world with his magic. He used the darkness to walk between realms, and it was mesmerizing, almost. How beautiful it was. His magic might have frightened people—but not me. Never me.

"Home," he murmured, the sound low under his breath.

I love you. I almost missed it, but I knew in my heart that he said it. Could feel the way he felt it, too.

The shadows wrapped around us, taking us back.

Taking us home.

I love you too, I sent back through our tether.

I felt defeated, like I'd lost something today. It hurt to think about Luna not being here whenever I needed her. She was my little sister, my twin flame—but more than that, she was my best friend. The one who knew me better than anyone else. The sister I'd do anything for.

But looking up at Damien as we stood in front of the old Victorian manor I called home, I realized I hadn't lost everything at all.

Because he was still here.

And we were home.

And... he loved me. I loved him.

I stared at the pumpkins sitting on the front porch. They'd lasted through the end of Halloween, the tree he'd carved for me and the cat I'd carved for him.

I didn't know what would happen next, what was coming for us in the future, but at least we'd be together.

Where we belonged.

damien

H*ome*. Pleasant Grove was my home now. Officially.

I stared up at Willow's family house. Our house now, I supposed.

As long as she wanted to stay here, I'd be here. She didn't know it yet, but I had a long future planned for us. An eternity together.

Picking her up in my arms—one of my hands on her back, and the other under her knees, I carried her over the threshold of the house.

Our house.

But when I turned to my witch, expecting happiness, she had a frown on her face.

"What is it, little witch?" I asked her, brushing the hair out of her face. Cupping her cheeks as she turned to face me. "I thought you'd be happy to be home. Together."

"I am, it's just..." Her eyes were glassy. "I didn't think about it till now. I don't want you to watch me grow old. To die. You'll live..." Willow's voice stuttered.

A long time. I knew it. A long lifespan was just one of the many things that came with being a demon.

"Willow," I murmured. "I don't have to watch you grow old." I interlaced one of her hands in mine, kissing her knuckles.

"We don't?" She blinked. "But I'm *mortal*. Practically human. I won't live as long as you."

"We can tether your life force to mine. Ensure that when we take our last breaths, it's together."

"Really?" She blinked away her tears. "So I'd live..."

"As long as I do, yes."

Willow wandered over to look out the window, like she was looking at the town. I wondered if she was thinking about the people here that she loved.

"You wouldn't age. At least, not normally. But we... could stay here. For as long as you'd want."

"We could?"

"I know what this place means to you. How much you love these people. It's your home."

"And Luna..." Her words trailed off, but I knew what she meant.

When Luna married my brother, she'd go through something similar. As the future Queen of the Demon realm, she would live by my brother's side for an eternity. "Yes."

"What about... kids?"

I blinked. "What?"

"I don't even know if you *want* to have kids, but would they..."

"Live as long as us?" I asked her. Sure, children of demons and witches weren't the most common, but they weren't rare. Plenty of demons had mated with humans and brought them back to our world. She gave a slight nod. "They would. They'd inherit magic from both of us."

We'd never had a chance to talk about having kids, about the little witch that had been in my dreams.

"I want that," I murmured, directly into her hair. "A family, with you."

"You do?" The tears were back, only this time—they were happy.

"Yes. Fuck yes, Willow. I want to do it all with you. Every little thing I've never experienced—I want to try it all with you. I want to see your world. To take you everywhere possible. And then show you mine." I squeezed her hands.

"I want that, too," she said, letting the tears fall. "An eternity with you."

"Thank fuck," I responded, taking her mouth. Kissing her, showing her how much I loved her with one simple action. "I love you."

She laughed. "I'm never going to get tired of hearing you say that."

"We don't have to do the ceremony now. We can wait." I thought about the jeweled ring in my back pocket. The one that had been my mom's. The same one she'd enchanted to protect me. "Do it at the same time as our wedding."

"Our wedding?" This time, she looked confused.

I laughed, bringing our foreheads together. "I know it hasn't been very long. That we still have so much to learn about each other. But, when the time comes.... I want to make you my wife. I want you to be mine in every way possible."

I could feel her smile against my mouth as we kissed again.

"Yes," she said as she pulled away, "Yes, I want to be your wife. All of it."

"I love you, Willow."

"I love you too, Damien."

I rubbed my fingers over her mark. "Mine," I murmured.

"Yours," she agreed.

Throwing her over my shoulder unceremoniously, I carted her from the living room into her bedroom.

"Damien!" Willow shrieked, dangling down my back. "You're ridiculous."

I dropped her on the bed, enjoying the way her eyes widened as I stood over her, stripping off my clothes.

"I've wanted you again since yesterday. Since I put my mark on you." Fuck, I'd never imagined how much I'd like it to see those two little imprints on her bare neck. Knowing that I put them there. "We didn't have enough time this morning."

The ballroom had eased the urge that the claiming had brought on, but it wasn't enough. Some males fucked for practically a week straight afterwards.

She bit her lip, watching me from lidded eyes.

"Like what you see?" I asked, smirking, knowing my full chest was on display as I unbuttoned my pants.

Her cheeks pinked, her hands moving to cover her eyes. "I wasn't watching."

"Willow." Grasping her fingers, I pulled them away from her face before pinning them to the bed, our hands intertwined. "Baby, you're allowed to look." Placing a kiss underneath her ear, I slipped my hands under her top, cupping her tits even through her lacy bra. I brushed my finger over a nipple, enjoying the shudder her body made from the sensation. "Because I'm *yours.*"

Willow squirmed underneath me. "*Please,*" she pleaded, even if she didn't know what for. I was happy to oblige. But first—

"You're wearing too many clothes," I muttered, fumbling with the hem of the sage green sweater she'd pulled on this morning.

"Take them off then," she agreed, before bringing her mouth back to mine.

We pulled apart long enough for me to whip her sweater off, dropping it on the floor behind me before rolling her leggings off of her legs. Stripped down to her orange polka dot panties and black lace bra, she'd never looked so much like *mine*.

I chuckled, kissing the top of each hip bone. "Cute panties." Her cheeks pinked, turning almost the same color as her little pink nipples. "I'm fucking obsessed with them." Hooking my thumbs into the waistband, I dragged them down her skin, not stopping until she was bare for me, exposing that perfect mound. "Obsessed with *you*."

When I'd gotten her back to my room last night, my cum had still been dripping out of her, and I'd almost lost it right then and there. But she'd been so tired, and all I'd wanted to do was take care of her. So I'd gotten her cleaned up and tucked her into bed.

But tonight, I was going to take my time. Maybe start working towards that eventual witchling. Whenever she decided to go off birth control, I couldn't fucking wait.

Unsnapping her bra, I took a moment to enjoy the view of her tits and that creamy skin.

"Can't get over how fucking perfect these are," I said. They were just begging for my mouth, and I couldn't resist tasting her. Moving my head down, I sucked one into my mouth. Lavishing it with attention, I swirled my tongue in circles over and over before switching to the other breast.

"Damien," she whined. "I need—"

I ran my fingers over the soft skin of her thighs, leaving a trail of goosebumps in their wake. Her sweet smell lingered in the air as I leaned back, taking in the sight of her. "I know what you need, baby." I kissed the swell of her breasts.

Standing up, I pushed my pants and briefs off in one clean motion, and my cock sprang to attention. I'd never get over the way Willow's eyes widened every time she saw me.

I eased inside of her without preamble—no foreplay. Still,

she was soaked for me, and I squeezed my eyes at the sensation of being inside her bare. Somehow, it got better every time. I was fucking lost in her, and I knew it.

"I love you," I murmured, capturing her lips as she wound her arms around my neck.

She moaned my name as I pulled out slightly, pushing in deeper.

This time, I'd go slow. I'd savor it. There was time for the rest, later.

I wanted her to know how much I loved her. Cherished her.

I kept up that pace, slow slides inside of her, until she was trembling against me, begging me for more.

"Tell me you're mine," I murmured again, kissing her bite.

"I'm yours," she agreed, her hips rocking in time to meet my shallow thrusts. Each time I hit her cervix, I felt a shudder run through her entire body. She was close, and I just needed her to let go.

I'd be right behind her, always.

"Come for me, baby."

"Damien," she cried. "I love you."

Bringing our mouths together, I kissed her deeply, letting go of everything else. "I love you," I murmured.

I used my shadows to apply pressure to her clit, and that was all it took. She came, squeezing around my cock, her insides milking me.

That was what tipped me over the edge, and I came on a cry of her name. Every last drop was spilled inside of her, leaving me boneless.

I buried my head against her breasts as I held her, feeling myself growing soft inside of her.

And even then, we remained connected.

"I can't wait for a lifetime of *that*," she laughed.
I pinched her cute little bare ass. "An eternity."
"Mmm. Forever sounds perfect with you."
It really did.
I couldn't wait to start the rest of our forever—together.

epilogue

Two years later...

A little tiny hand tugged at a black tail. Because, for whatever reason, my *husband* thought it was absolutely adorable to continue shifting into his cat form even when we had things to do.

"Damien." I narrowed my eyes at him.

Meow. He wiggled his butt, tail swishing back and forth as he prevented the chubby little fingers from grabbing it.

"Opal." I sighed, scooping our nine-month-old daughter into my arms. "We don't play with Daddy."

I heard a chuckling sound and the padding of feet coming from our room.

"What—" I looked at Damien, and then at the black cat at our daughter's feet. "If you're not... Then..."

Opal giggled as the cat brushed against her legs, her dark curls bouncing from the motion. She'd gotten his hair, long and thick and black as night. But she had my bright green eyes, and of course—my fondness for cats.

I'd never gotten around to getting another familiar after Damien turned out to *not* be a cat, but I didn't mind. The two-for-one special I'd gotten with my feline companion also being my mate, had worked out pretty well.

And when our little bundle of joy had come, I'd knew our family was perfect.

The spring after we'd met, I'd spent a week unable to keep anything down, and when Luna had come for a visit, she'd taken one look at me and she *knew*. Even before I did. A fact that never ceased to irritate me.

Leveling a glare at my husband, I crossed my arms over my chest. I might have loved him, but I was also peeved at him. "Why, exactly, is there a strange cat in my house?"

He leaned down, kissing me on the lips gently. "Hello to you too, Wil."

I ran my fingers over the wedding band on his left hand. We'd gotten married a year ago, in a small ceremony held in the town's gazebo. I'd been six months pregnant at the time, but we hadn't wanted to wait.

After Opal had been born, we'd had a second ceremony— this time in the demon realm, but with a lot more fanfare.

All I'd cared about was the man at the end of the aisle and the tiny baby who'd slept in her aunt's arms. The rest of it didn't matter.

"Are we just... ignoring that?" I waved at the strange cat.

"Oh, Zain just wanted to drop in and say hello," he said, grinning. "He brought Opal a friend."

"Zain's here?" My eyes lit up. "Did he bring Luna with him?"

Damien brushed his nose against mine. "Of course he did."

But before I could let myself relax into the gesture, I raised an eyebrow, looking back at the cat.

"Relax." He placed a kiss on my forehead. "She's *just* a cat, I promise."

Better be, I sent the thought through our bond. *Or you're on the couch tonight.* I didn't need any more demons masquerading as cats in our lives.

Damien was enough. He was more than enough. He was everything.

He smirked, holding out a hand. "Shall we?"

"What do you think, Opal? Want to go visit Auntie Luna?"

My baby girl gave me a big, toothy grin, and I happily scooped her up into my arms, placing kisses all over her soft skin.

I didn't get to see my sister as much these days—mostly on account of her marriage to the literal Demon King. Another advancement of the last two years, after the death of Damien's father.

We'd both stepped back from the bakery, hiring on a new head baker and a manager.

I hadn't realized that while I was wondering what my path was in life, so was Luna. But she seemed happy, and I couldn't judge. Not when I'd fallen in love with a demon myself.

I hadn't quite decided what was next in life. I'd planned on getting another job after stepping back from the bakery, but then I'd gotten pregnant with Opal. And I decided I liked the role of Mom better than anything else I could have ever dreamed of.

I still dabbled in potions, and these days, I had a whole slew of witches requesting different cures for their ailments. It felt like they had a newfound awe for me after they'd found out about me breaking my demon's curse.

He'd settled into his role as a resident of Pleasant Grove, but more importantly, into being a father. Even though he sometimes still shapeshifted into cat form and let our toddler play with him.

Damien still rolled his eyes when I called it *Hell*—but after visiting quite a few times, I had to admit it had its own charms.

Like the *giant* bathtub that took up almost an entire room, or the king sized bed that was so decadent I never wanted to get out of it. Damien's *suites* were lavish and lush and the perfect escape from life.

And then there was his house—the one that barely deserved to be called that. It was basically a mansion, built onto a large piece of property outside of the demon capital.

When you live a long time, you have a lot of money saved up. He'd shrugged. *I figured it would be an excellent investment.*

And one day, it would be our home. After we'd raised Opal with the witches, let her choose her path—then we'd retire to the demon realm for the rest of our eternity.

I liked the sound of it more and more every day.

Forever with the man—the demon—that I loved.

And the baby girl who'd brought so much joy into my life.

With the sister I'd given up everything for, who'd found her own path.

My family was complete. Mine. Perfect.

My demon smiled up at me, taking Opal from my arms. "Come to daddy, baby girl." He brushed a hand over her little black curls.

Part of me—part of him. She'd gotten my eyes. And a tiny splattering of freckles on her cheeks. The rest, though, was all Damien. His complexion, the onyx hue of her hair.

We could always make another one, you know, he said, watching me watch them. *It might be fun.*

She's not even a year old yet. What's the rush?

He gave me a little smirk. *What? I like seeing you pregnant.*

"Mommy and Daddy need to give you a little sister, huh, Opal?" He grinned, bouncing our little girl up in the air.

"How are you so sure it won't be a boy?" I furrowed my brow.

He laughed. "I just have this feeling."

I rubbed over my wedding ring—the ring that used to be his mother's—thinking about our family. Not yet, but... I liked the idea of adding another member to our family soon.

After Halloween was over, maybe we could start thinking about it. But I wanted to enjoy my baby girl's first Halloween. I'd already bought the cutest costume, and we were all going to match.

Besides, what were the odds he'd knock me up on the first try, anyway?

I adjusted her little jumper.

"Shall we?" He asked.

But I know he didn't just mean going to see Luna and Zain.

"Yes," I agreed.

To the future. To our life. To our family.

To every blissfully perfect moment that would come, and every single one in between.

I'd never expected to find my perfect man, let alone a demon. Never imagined that the cat I'd adopted would have been the male the fates picked for me. My mate.

And yet, here I was. Living my perfect life. It was everything I'd ever wanted, and everything I'd never known how to wish for.

"I love you," I murmured, pressing a soft kiss to his lips, before leaning in to kiss our daughter's cheek.

"I love you, too, little witch," he agreed, returning one back. "Both of you."

The End.

coming next halloween...

Wickedly Yours
Fall 2024
Luna & Zain's Story
Tropes: Fated Mates, Marriage of Convenience, Witch x
Demon, Royalty

Keep reading for a sneak peek of Chapter One!

wickedly yours

LUNA

Ghoul's Night

    I'd never believed in the *tall, dark, and handsome stranger* stereotype before. And yet, the man standing at the edge of the bar was equally all three.

There was a part of me that wanted to do a one-eighty and run. That saw the beautiful man and thought, *turn around, Luna. Look the other way and don't go over there.*

But I'd never been good at listening to my intuition. No matter how good it was.

I'd always been the kind of girl who kept looking forward. *What was next?* That was the question I'd been asking myself for the last year.

I loved my life in Pleasant Grove, the bakery I ran with my sister and having all of my coven at my side.

But something was missing.

My older sister, Willow, was on the dance floor, dancing with her new man, Damien. She was trying to play it off that there was nothing between them, but the way they looked at each other... it was obvious what was growing between them.

I was happy for her. If anyone deserved love and a happy

ending, it was Willow. After our parents had died in an accident, she'd graduated college and come back to town, forsaking her own dream to help me start mine.

The Witches' Brew wouldn't have existed without *both* of us. Willow had always been skilled at brewing potions, and she translated that to brewing the *best* coffee drinks in our entire town. I wasn't biased, either. Everyone came in the mornings to get a drink from her.

Her recipes were magical. I'd loved our time being in business together, even if it was coming to a close. I could feel it.

Willow liked to say that I was a *seer,* but I'd never really thought of myself like that. I'd never experienced visions or anything of the sort—just feelings, and general premonitions.

And yet, tonight...

The man sipped from a glass of whiskey and I slid off my stool, my feet hitting the floor before I'd even made my decision yet.

That was the funny thing about fate. It hit you when you were least expecting it.

Maybe I'd never see him again. But maybe...

"Hi," I said, adjusting my lavender colored dress. The skirt was sewn to look like a spiderweb, with each seam coming to a point.

What was the point of coming to a themed night at The Enchanted Cauldron and not dressing to theme?

Ghoul's Night was the quintessential spooky night at the bar, but I'd never been a witch who loved the color black or jewel tones. Pastels were more my speed.

The dark-haired man raised his eyebrow as he looked at me, like he was appraising me. Just one look, and a shiver ran through me.

"Hello." His voice was deep—a baritone I didn't hear often on the men in this town.

It was hot. Sexy, even. I bit my lip as I slid onto the stool next to him, setting my drink down on the counter.

"Come here often?" I asked, taking a sip of my Poison Apple Martini.

He chuckled, the deep sound reverberating through me. "No. This is a first."

"Ah." I wasn't even trying to hide the fact that I was staring at him. "Are you just passing through?"

Pleasant Grove was a well-warded community. Since normal humans had no clue that *magic* or witches even existed, most patrons here were magical themselves.

"You could say that."

"What else could you say?"

"That I'm looking for something."

"And did you find it?"

He looked directly at me, those dark eyes—almost black, practically peering into my soul. "I think I did."

"Oh." I took another drink, bobbing my head. "That's good."

The handsome stranger set his empty drink glass down on the bar. "Yes. Yes, it is." He flashed me a dazzling smile, offering his hand to me. "Hi. I'm Zain."

"Luna," I answered, putting my hand in his to shake it.

"It's nice to meet you, Luna," Zain murmured, kissing my knuckles.

The alcohol must have been affecting my system more than I thought, because I *giggled*. I actually giggled.

Was I drunk? I peered at my empty glass.

Looking back up at the Zain—my handsome stranger—I found myself getting lost in his eyes.

"Do you want to get out of here?" I murmured, placing the glass back down on the bar.

I'd never been so bold before, but there was something about him... Something that intrigued me.

Something that I wanted to get to know.

And when he slipped his hand in mine, everything just felt... right.

To be continued next Halloween...

acknowledgments

Happy Halloween, Witches!

This book was so fun for me to write, partially because it was completely different than anything else I've written before. I let the story take me where it wanted to, and I had so much fun letting Willow and Damien take the lead.

To Katie W, Katie D, Arzum, Gabbi Autumn, & Gwen: I love you all very much. Thank you for your never-ending support and love for me with this (and all) of my books.

To you, the readers. Thank you so much for taking a chance on this book and with Willow and Damien. I hope you fell in love with them the way I have.

To my parents: thank you for supporting me. As always: giant thank you for not reading this book.

also by jennifer chipman

Best Friends Book Club

Academically Yours - Noelle & Matthew

Disrespectfully Yours - Angelina & Benjamin

Fearlessly Yours - Gabrielle & Hunter

Gracefully Yours - Charlotte & Daniel

Contractually Yours - Nicolas & Zofia (TBD)

Castleton University

A Not-So Prince Charming - Ella & Cameron (TBD)

Holiday Standalones

Spookily Yours - Willow & Damien

Wickedly Yours - Luna & Zain (coming Fall 2024)

about the author

Originally from the Portland area, Jennifer now lives in Orlando with her dog, Walter and cat, Max. She always has her nose in a book and loves going to the Disney Parks in her free time.

Website: www.jennchipman.com

a amazon.com/author/jenniferchipman
g goodreads.com/jennchipman
◎ instagram.com/jennchipmanauthor
f facebook.com/jennchipmanauthor
X x.com/jennchipman
♪ tiktok.com/@jennchipman
ⓟ pinterest.com/jennchipmanauthor

Printed in Great Britain
by Amazon

41764565R00134